Book © 1994 by Running Press

COPYRIGHT OFFICE COPY NOV 1 6 1994 LIBRARY OF CONGRESS

W9-DAW-706

f Dinosaurs

Tuojiangosaurus
Elmisaurus?
Struthiomimus
Plateosaurus
Orodromeus
Triceratops
Velociraptor

The Age of

Archaeopteryx
Tyrannosaurus
Oviraptor
Yaverlandia
Panoplosaurus
Pisanosaurus?

Brachios
Lambeosaurus
Troodon
Anchisaurus
Allosaurus
Psittacosaurus
Spinosaurus
Herrerasaurus

START EXPLORING™

The Age of Dinosaurs

A Fact-Filled Coloring Book

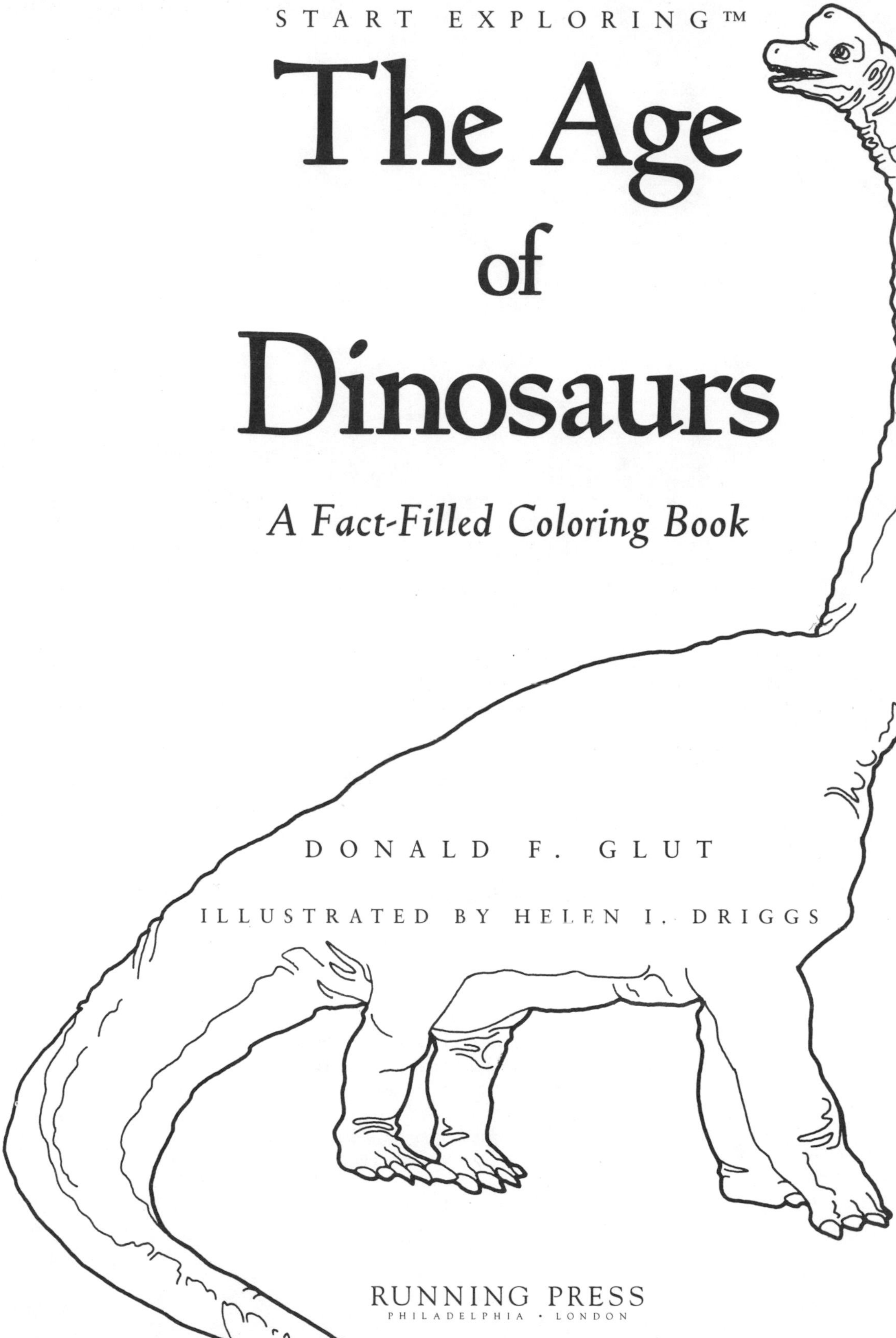

DONALD F. GLUT

ILLUSTRATED BY HELEN I. DRIGGS

RUNNING PRESS
PHILADELPHIA • LONDON

Copyright © 1994 by Running Press Book Publishers.
All rights reserved under the Pan-American and International Copyright Conventions.

This book may not be reproduced in whole or in part in any form or by any means, electronic or mechanical, including photocopying, recording, or by any information storage and retrieval system now known or hereafter invented, without written permission from the publisher.

Canadian representatives: General Publishing Co., Ltd.,
30 Lesmill Road, Don Mills, Ontario M3B 2T6.

9 8 7 6 5 4 3 2 1
Digit on the right indicates the number of this printing.

ISBN 1-56138-456-9

Cover design: E. June Roberts
Interior design: Susan Van Horn and Ken Newbaker
Editor: David Borgenicht
Cover, interior, and poster illustrations: Helen I. Driggs
Poster copyright © 1994 by Running Press Book Publishers
Typography: Truesdell and Sabon by Deborah Lugar
Printed in Canada

This book may be ordered by mail from the publisher.
Please add $2.50 for postage and handling.
But try your bookstore first!
Running Press Book Publishers
125 South Twenty-second Street
Philadelphia, Pennsylvania 19103-4399

CONTENTS

Part One: ***Meet the Dinosaurs***

Part Two: ***The Lizard-Hipped Dinosaurs***

Part Three: ***The Bird-Hipped Dinosaurs***

Part Four: ***Beyond the Bones***

PART ONE:

Meet the Dinosaurs

Introduction

Dinosaurs were among the most successful animals that ever lived.

For 150 million years, they lived almost everywhere land-dwelling animals could, on every continent, in many different kinds of environments. They were fantastic in appearance—many of them were spectacular creatures every bit as bizarre as the monsters of mythology or the imagined inhabitants of alien worlds.

But none of us will ever see a dinosaur in the flesh because the last of these animals perished some 64 million years ago. For that reason, they are all the more intriguing.

Hundreds of dinosaur species have been discovered, named, and classified during the last 150 years. We know them from the remains (called fossils) that they left behind.

Yet although we have learned much about how dinosaurs looked when they were alive, we will probably never know their color. That's where you come in. The black-and-white pictures in this book are waiting for your

imagination. You can read, then decide for yourself what they looked like.

The world of dinosaurs awaits.

Dinosaur Basics

Their scientific name is Dinosauria, which means "terrible lizards," but the dinosaurs were not lizards—and not all prehistoric reptiles were dinosaurs.

All dinosaurs were alike in certain ways. Dinosaurs did not creep or crawl, like lizards and crocodiles do. The pelvis, leg, ankle, and foot bones of all dinosaurs allowed them to stand upright, like mammals. And all dinosaurs lived on land. (Flying reptiles or pterosaurs, and marine reptiles like plesiosaurs, mosasaurs, and ichthyosaurs, were not dinosaurs, although they lived at the same time.)

Dinosaurs belong to a larger group of "ruling reptiles," called Archosauria. Flying reptiles, like the small *Ramphorynchus* and giant *Pteranodon*, and crocodilians, both prehistoric and modern, are also "ruling reptiles" and are related to the dinosaurs.

The dinosaurs may have descended from an animal like *Euparkaria*, a reptile that lived long before the earliest dinosaurs. This 5-foot long animal had a relatively large head (about 9 inches long), and walked on its hind legs. This animal resembled some of the earliest meat-eating dinosaurs, and was a preview of what was to come.

The Dinosaur Trail

Without fossils, we would not know that dinosaurs (or any other extinct life forms) ever existed.

"Fossil" literally means "dug up." Dinosaur fossils include physical remains such as preserved bones and skin prints, and even traces (such as footprints, eggs, and dung). But the most collected dinosaur specimens are bones, which turned to stone, or petrified, through the long process of fossilization.

How did dinosaur bones become fossilized? First, a dead dinosaur somehow fell or was washed into a body of water, usually a river or lake. There the bones were buried by clay or sand called *sediment* in the water. After thousands or sometimes millions of years, the organic matter of the bones was replaced by minerals as water passed through the sediment. Eventually most or all of the bones' original matter was replaced so the bones became petrified.

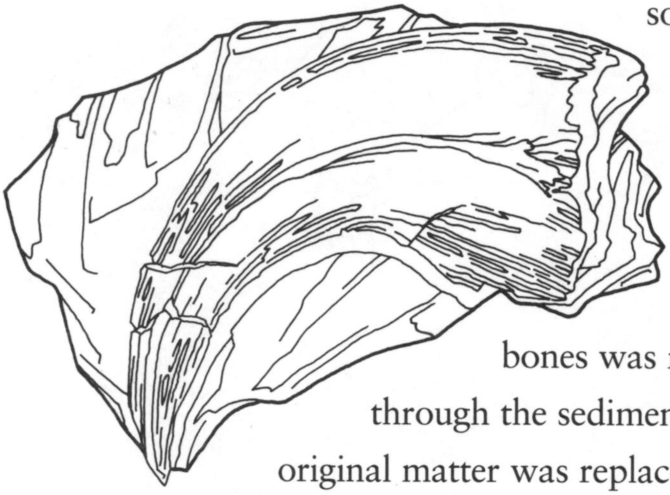

Only in rare cases are complete (or nearly complete) dinosaur skeletons found. Many dinosaurs are known only from a few pieces of fossil. Some dinosaurs have been named based upon the discovery of only a partial bone, or fossil scrap. In fact, most dinosaur skeletons on display are at least partially incomplete and had to be reconstructed with bones from other species or resculptured.

Fossils are vital clues to the great mystery that is the history of Earth. They are pieces of a vast puzzle that will probably never be complete—but it's a challenge to try.

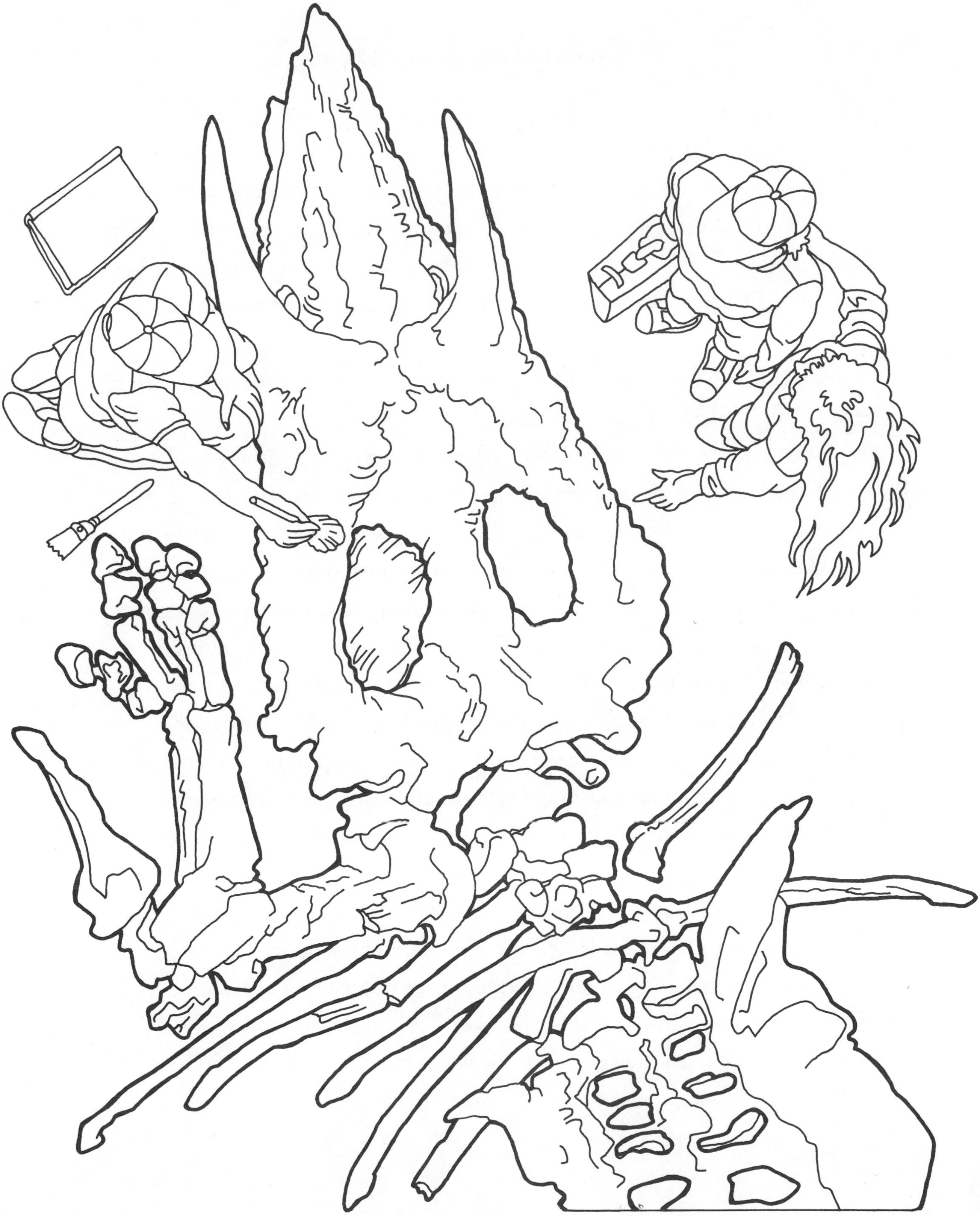

Dinosaur Hunters

The science of ancient living beings, called paleontology, is the study of fossils. Dinosaur fossils are studied by vertebrate paleontologists, scientists who study animals that have backbones. These are the dinosaur hunters.

Most paleontologists have years of training in their subject and in other fields of science such as geology and biology. However, important work has been done by so-called "amateurs." Some of our most spectacular dinosaur discoveries have been made by non-paleontologists. The biggest known dinosaur, *seismosaurus*, was discovered in 1979, by three amateurs—Arthur Loy, Frank Walker, Jan Cummings, and Bill Norlander.

Paleontologists do different kinds of work. Some work in the field and spend much of their time searching for and collecting fossils. Once the fossils have been collected and prepared, the paleontologists may write up formal descriptions of them, which are published in scientific journals. If the fossils introduce a new animal, the paleontologist gives it a new name.

Some paleontologists do most of their work indoors, at museums or universities. Others teach, paving the way for future dinosaur hunters.

One thing is certain: Every paleontologist has a keen interest in the history of life on Earth. He or she knows how to interpret the evidence of fossils and can use imagination to bring the creatures back to life.

If you were a paleontologist, how would you know where to look for dinosaur fossils? You wouldn't just go out somewhere and start digging. First, you look for rocks that are from about 64 to 248 million years old, the right age for dinosaurs. (There are a number of scientific ways to determine this, including calculating the rate of decay of a rock's radioactive isotopes.) In the U.S., the most likely places to look would be Utah, Nevada, Montana, Colorado, Wyoming, New Mexico, South Dakota, Oklahoma, and Texas.

Then you'd look for places where you could see bare rock, which results from erosion, quarrying, or other damaging forces. Rocks with bone chips lying on the surface or bones imbedded in the rock itself signal that more bones may be buried underground.

Fossil bones are usually cracked and brittle, so paleontologists apply various glues and resins to strengthen them before removal. They also use chipping and digging tools (and sometimes explosives) to carefully free the bones. Once removed, the bones are usually wrapped in burlap jackets and protected in plaster.

In a preparation laboratory, usually at a museum or university, the protective jackets are opened, and the fossils are removed from the surrounding rock. Extracting the fossils from the rock is slow and time-consuming and can take several hours, days, or even years.

This is done using hand tools like needles, electrical devices like small drills, and even acid. Only after the fossil has been prepared (first strengthened, then exposed or removed from the rock), can it be studied.

Most dinosaur fossils remain in a museum or university's collections for study. Others are put on exhibit for the public to see and appreciate.

That explains *how* we know about these remarkable creatures. Here's some of what we know.

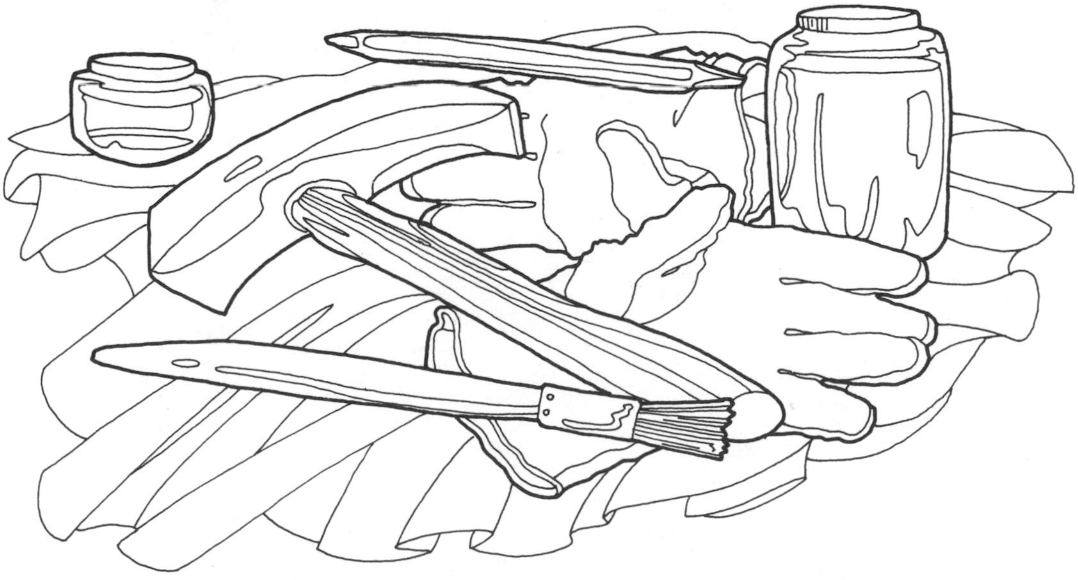

TOROSAURUS

The Dinosaur World: The Mesozoic Era

The dinosaurs lived during "middle life"—the Mesozoic Era, a period of time that lasted from about 248 million years to 64 million years ago. Because Earth's lands, seas, and skies were dominated by reptiles during the Mesozoic, it is known as the "Age of Reptiles."

The geography of Earth in the Mesozoic Era was very different from that of today. During this era, the world's present-day continents were all a part of one huge supercontinent called Pangaea. Moving on great sheets of Earth's crust called *tectonic plates* and floating on magma heated by the Earth's core, the continents broke apart, shifting a few inches each Mesozoic year to where they are today. Even today, the continents shift a fraction of an inch per year.

Geologists divide the Mesozoic Era into three periods—the Triassic (245 to 208 million years ago), the Jurassic (203 to 145.6 million years ago), and the Cretaceous (144 to 64 million years ago).

The Triassic was a warm period, dominated by many different and exotic reptiles, especially big, long-snouted crocodile-like creatures, called phytosaurs. The dinosaurs made their debut in the Late Triassic. During the Jurassic, the climate was somewhat cooler, and old mountain ranges eroded away. By the Cretaceous, distinct seasons started occurring, and new mountains formed. The end of the Cretaceous period marked the end of the dinosaurs' reign.

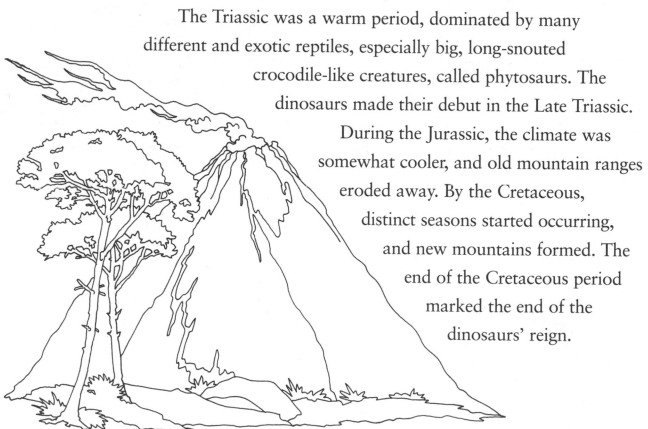

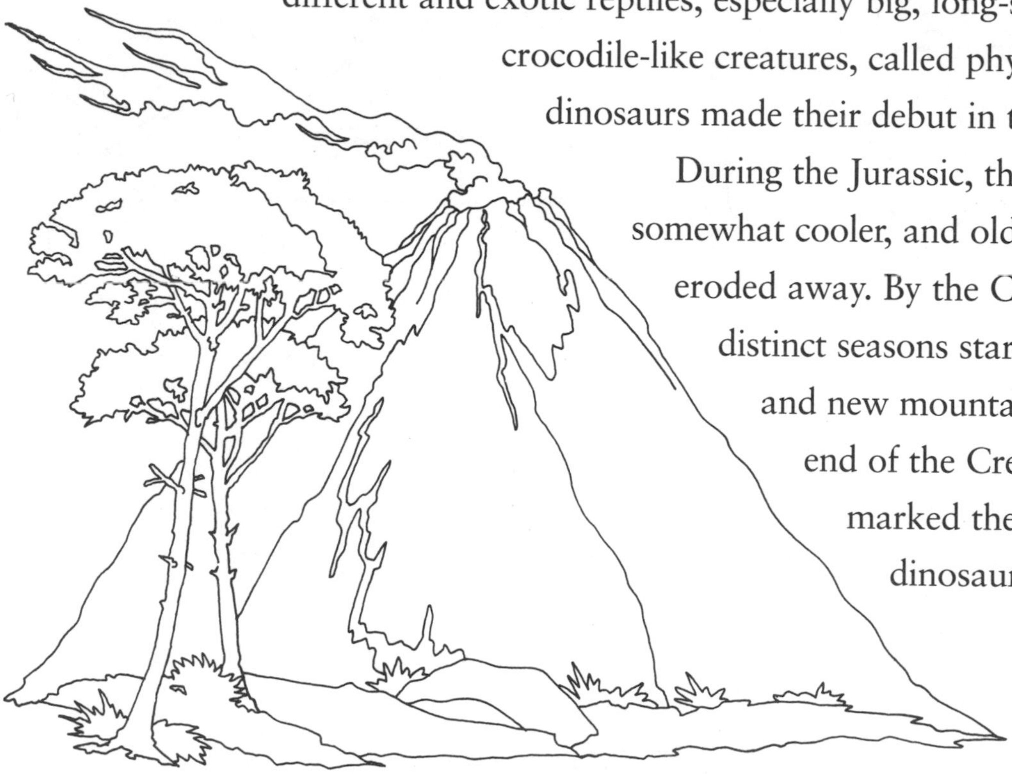

PART TWO:

The Lizard-Hipped Dinosaurs

Saurischia: The Lizard Hips

There are two major dinosaur groups—Saurischia and Ornithischia.

The Saurischia are called "lizard-hipped" dinosaurs, even though dinosaurs are not closely related to lizards. Saurischian dinosaurs were named for the arrangement of their pelvic bones—in the saurischian pelvis, as in a lizard's, the three pelvic bones (the ilium, ischium, and pubis) radiate away from one another in different directions. This is just one major difference between saurischians and ornithischians or "bird-hipped dinosaurs."

Saurischians first appeared during the Late Triassic period and thrived until the Late Cretaceous. They ranged in size from the smallest of all dinosaurs (chicken-sized, like *Compsognathus*) to the most gigantic (more than 100 feet long, like *Seismosaurus*).

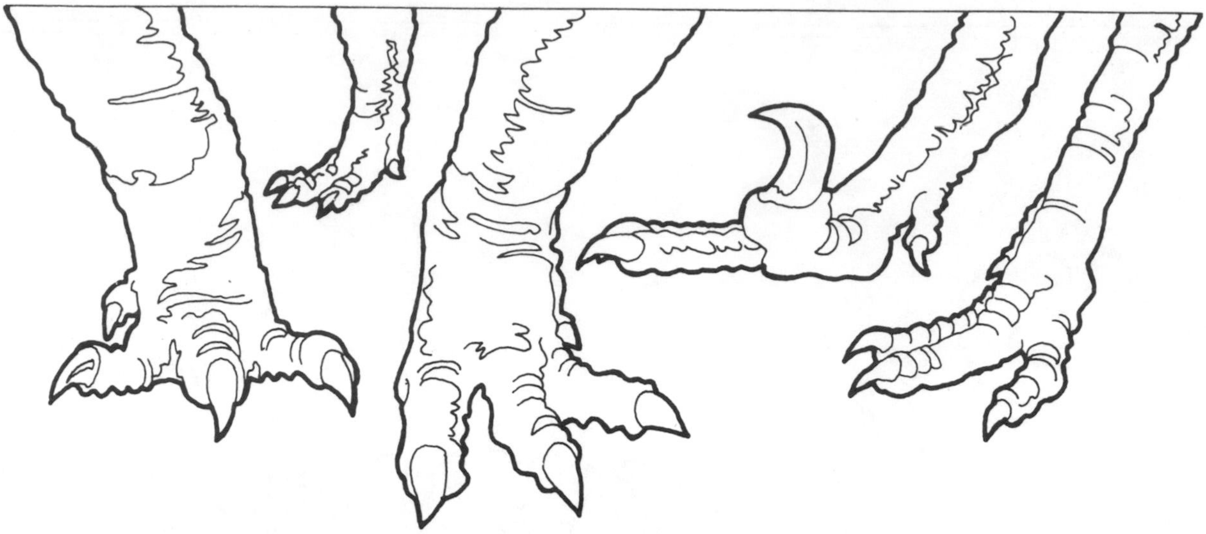

Beast Feet

The first group of lizard-hipped dinosaurs to appear was the Theropoda, or "beast feet."

Actually, their feet were not really "beast-like." They were more birdlike, with a small first toe that looked like a spur. Theropod dinosaurs probably walked on their hind legs—skeletons show that their front legs were too short for them to walk on all fours.

Although a small number of theropods were toothless, most had mouths lined with sharp teeth. Almost all theropods were meat-eaters (carnivores) and ate other animals, insects, and eggs. A few of them may have been plant-eaters (herbivores) or dinosaurs that ate both meat and plants (omnivores). Theropods were the only dinosaurs known to eat meat and were active hunters and scavengers.

The role of theropods in the food chain can be compared to that of lions, tigers, wolves, and other meat-eating animals of today. They preyed upon plant-eaters, keeping their numbers in check. Even today, without carnivores, the world would be overrun by herbivores!

The First Dinosaurs

As far as we know, Eoraptor, "the dawn thief," was the earliest and most primitive theropod—and the oldest dinosaur.

It was a small meat-eater, but a clever hunter forced by its size to prey mainly upon small animals. In bold moments, it may have snatched up the young of larger animals—but Eoraptor had to be careful. The main meat-eaters of its day were narrow-nosed reptiles called phytosaurs, some of which grew to more than 19 feet long, six times longer than Eoraptor. Dinosaurs were secondary citizens of their world at this time—it was not yet their turn to rule the Earth.

Soon after the debut of Eoraptor, a group of theropods called Herrerasauridae appeared. Like many theropods, the members of this group, Herrerasaurus and Staurikosaurus, had large heads, sharp teeth, short necks, and long thighs. Their forelimbs were long compared to their hindlimbs.

Dino Facts

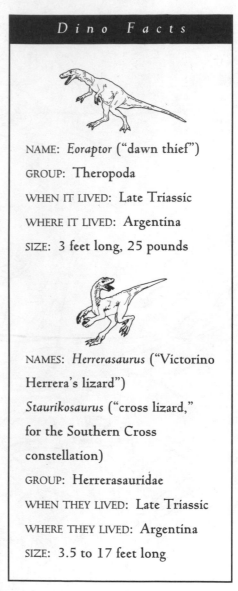

NAME: *Eoraptor* ("dawn thief")
GROUP: Theropoda
WHEN IT LIVED: Late Triassic
WHERE IT LIVED: Argentina
SIZE: 3 feet long, 25 pounds

NAMES: *Herrerasaurus* ("Victorino Herrera's lizard")
Staurikosaurus ("cross lizard," for the Southern Cross constellation)
GROUP: Herrerasauridae
WHEN THEY LIVED: Late Triassic
WHERE THEY LIVED: Argentina
SIZE: 3.5 to 17 feet long

Both of these dinosaurs were small. Their small ear bones suggest that they probably had a keen sense of hearing, which would have been an advantage to small animals in a world still dominated by large meat-eating reptiles. A hungry Staurikosaurus or Herrerasaurus must have bolted away from its intended prey when it heard an even hungrier phytosaur coming.

Herrerasaurids were agile, quick-moving creatures. We know this because their thigh bones were shorter than their lower-leg bones, indications of running animals. Their foreclaws were well designed for catching prey. Holding their victims in their hinged jaws, these early dinosaurs tore into its flesh with long, serrated teeth.

Horned Hunters

The Ceratosauria, or horned lizards, were primitive theropods, but these dinosaurs were far more advanced than their herrerasaurid cousins. They lived from the Late Triassic through the Late Cretaceous and ranged from several feet to 30 feet in length. Some had heads bearing fleshy horns or crests, which were probably used for display, like the horns of antelopes today.

One "horned lizard," a lightly-built animal with a rather long head, was called *Rioarribasaurus*. A "mass grave" of this dinosaur was found at Ghost Ranch, New Mexico. This quarry has yielded hundreds of skeletons. They show *Rioarribasaurus* examples from a baby to an adult, males and females.

One well-preserved skeleton included the skeleton of a juvenile in its stomach area. At first paleontologists wondered whether this

Dino Facts

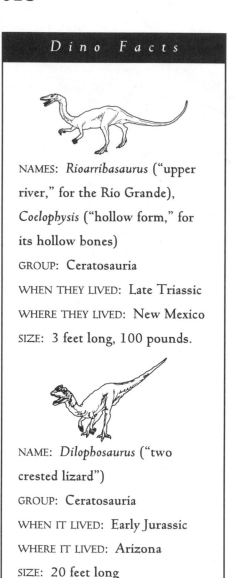

NAMES: *Rioarribasaurus* ("upper river," for the Río Grande), *Coelophysis* ("hollow form," for its hollow bones)
GROUP: Ceratosauria
WHEN THEY LIVED: Late Triassic
WHERE THEY LIVED: New Mexico
SIZE: 3 feet long, 100 pounds.

NAME: *Dilophosaurus* ("two crested lizard")
GROUP: Ceratosauria
WHEN IT LIVED: Early Jurassic
WHERE IT LIVED: Arizona
SIZE: 20 feet long

was the tiny skeleton of an unborn baby dinosaur. Then, they realized its bones were actually those of a young animal bigger than an infant—evidence that *Rioarribasaurus* was a cannibal. The number of skeletons taken from the Ghost Ranch site make this one of the best-known dinosaurs.

One of the earliest large theropods was *Dilophosaurus*. It had twin crests atop its head. These crests were quite fragile and were probably used for displays—a male may have used the size or color of its crests to attract females, as peacocks do with their feather displays. A proud male *Dilophosaurus* must have been an impressive sight, turning its head in the sunlight to show off its crests.

Ceratosaurus, a large ceratosaur, had a prominent nose horn. Because it needed no weapons other than its teeth, claws, and size, this horn was probably not used as a weapon. Male *Ceratosaurus* may have used their horns in butting contests over territory and mates.

Recently discovered ceratosaurs include *Abelisaurus* and *Carnotaurus*. *Carnotaurus* had a very short face, short forelimbs, and two large "bull-like" horns. A male *Carnotaurus* may have used its horns to

Dino Facts

NAME: *Ceratosaurus* ("horned lizard")
GROUP: Ceratosauria
WHEN IT LIVED: Late Jurassic
WHERE IT LIVED: Colorado, Utah, Oklahoma, East Africa
SIZE: 20 to 30 feet long

NAME: *Abelisaurus* ("Roberto Abelís lizard")
GROUP: Ceratosauria
WHEN IT LIVED: Late Cretaceous
WHERE IT LIVED: Argentina
SIZE: Possibly 25 to 30 feet long

NAME: *Carnotaurus* ("meat-eating bull")
GROUP: Ceratosauria
WHEN IT LIVED: Early Cretaceous
WHERE IT LIVED: Argentina
SIZE: 20 feet long

intimidate other males, as do modern deer. The *Carnotaurus* with the largest "headgear" would have dominated the others.

Meat-Eating Lizards

The meat-eating lizards, or Carnosauria, were huge theropods with big heads, ornamentation (like small horns above their eyes), and large teeth. They had short necks atop barrel-like trunks. Their forelimbs were small, and their three-toed feet had claws.

The best known carnosaur is *Allosaurus*. From its 3-foot head, large mouth, saber-like 4–6 inch-long teeth, and powerful frame, we know *Allosaurus* was a powerful and dangerous predator. *Allosaurus* had small pronounced "horns" above its eyes, and it attacked its prey with its dangerous three-fingered hands—each finger equipped with a sharp, curved claw up to 6 inches long.

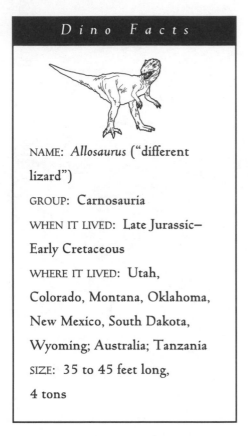

> ***Dino Facts***
>
> 
>
> NAME: *Allosaurus* ("different lizard")
>
> GROUP: Carnosauria
>
> WHEN IT LIVED: Late Jurassic–Early Cretaceous
>
> WHERE IT LIVED: Utah, Colorado, Montana, Oklahoma, New Mexico, South Dakota, Wyoming; Australia; Tanzania
>
> SIZE: 35 to 45 feet long, 4 tons

Most *Allosaurus* bones have been recovered from the Cleveland-Lloyd Dinosaur Quarry in Utah. Since 1927, the well-preserved remains of at least 44 *Allosaurus* individuals have been taken from this quarry.

Why was there such a large concentration of bones there? Perhaps because the animals were trapped during some kind of catastrophe—an earthquake or volcanic eruption. But the bones seem to have been scattered before burial, and there are also signs of scavenging, adding to the mystery of this fossil site. Scientists have yet to determine the truth—your guess is as

good as theirs.

Another carnosaur was *Acrocanthosaurus*. Unlike *Allosaurus* and many other theropods, which had their heads positioned at the end of their S-shaped necks, *Acrocanthosaurus's* head jutted forward from a straight neck. *Acrocanthosaurus* also had spines up to 17 inches long on its backbone. Their function is not known.

Dino Facts

NAME: *Acrocanthosaurus* ("high spined lizard")

GROUP: Carnosauria

WHEN IT LIVED: Early Cretaceous

WHERE IT LIVED: Oklahoma, Texas

SIZE: 40 feet long, 4 tons

Hollow Lizards

Most theropod dinosaurs fall into a subgroup of "hollow lizards," or Coelurosauria. They are named for their hollow bones. Coelurosaurs come in many shapes and with many interesting adaptations, and range in size from the very smallest to some of the biggest carnivorous dinosaurs of them all.

Chicken-sized *Compsognathus*, an early coelurosaur, is the smallest known dinosaur. One of the most complete and best-preserved dinosaur skeletons is a specimen of *Compsognathus*, discovered in limestone in Germany. The development of this specimen's bones show that it was a juvenile when it died—a mature adult would have been bigger. Preserved within the stomach area of this specimen was the skeleton of a small lizard, so we know what this *Compsognathus* individual enjoyed for its last meal. Information like this helps paleontologists better understand their subjects' lives. Tiny markings included in the rocks around this fossil have recently been identified as eggs, indicating that *Compsognathus*, like other dinosaurs, laid eggs to give birth.

Dino Facts

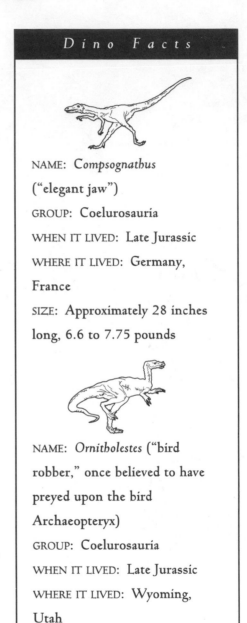

NAME: *Compsognathus* ("elegant jaw")
GROUP: Coelurosauria
WHEN IT LIVED: Late Jurassic
WHERE IT LIVED: Germany, France
SIZE: Approximately 28 inches long, 6.6 to 7.75 pounds

NAME: *Ornitholestes* ("bird robber," once believed to have preyed upon the bird Archaeopteryx)
GROUP: Coelurosauria
WHEN IT LIVED: Late Jurassic
WHERE IT LIVED: Wyoming, Utah
SIZE: 6 feet long

Ornitholestes was a much larger coelurosaur than *Compsognathus*. It was

a graceful, lightly-built animal with a long tail that helped to stabilize it when it ran after prey or from larger theropods. Its skull shows a trace of what may have been a small horn over its nose, which could have been used by males to attract mates or to win territory.

Killer Claws

The "killer claws," or Dromaeosauridae, a subgroup of Coelurosauria, were distinguished by the large sickle-shaped claws on their feet.

This group was named after Dromaeosaurus, the first discovered dinosaur of this kind. This small, sharp-toothed, fast-running hunter had a large, curved talon on the inner toe of each foot, a weapon for slashing prey. A relative of about the same size, Velociraptor, was found in Mongolia in the early 1920s. Both were vicious and dangerous hunters.

But the best known dromaeosaurid is *Deinonychus*. *Deinonychus* had a long tail, which it held out stiffly behind its body with a bundle of bony rods. This tail kept its body balanced when it walked or ran. Deinonychus was also a capable hunter—its eyesight was good—all the better to seek out its prey. The "killer claws" on its feet were designed as

Dino Facts

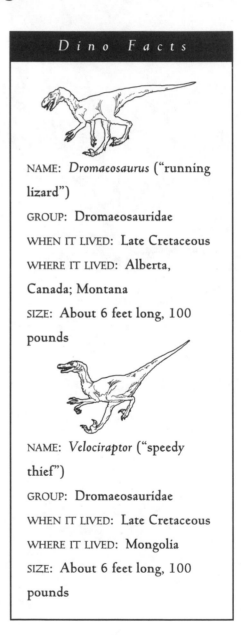

NAME: *Dromaeosaurus* ("running lizard")
GROUP: Dromaeosauridae
WHEN IT LIVED: Late Cretaceous
WHERE IT LIVED: Alberta, Canada; Montana
SIZE: About 6 feet long, 100 pounds

NAME: *Velociraptor* ("speedy thief")
GROUP: Dromaeosauridae
WHEN IT LIVED: Late Cretaceous
WHERE IT LIVED: Mongolia
SIZE: About 6 feet long, 100 pounds

deadly offensive weapons.

Deinonychus was an active and swift-moving animal. When it attacked, it gripped its prey tightly with its strong, three-fingered grasping hands. Then it finished the grisly job with a slash of its large foot claw.

Paleontologists found remains of *Deinonychus* mixed with those of the much larger plant-eating dinosaur *Tenontosaurus*. This suggests that *Deinonychus* hunted prey that was much larger than it was, stalking in packs like wolves and then working together to bring down a victim.

Dino Facts

NAME: *Deinonychus* ("terrible claw")

GROUP: Dromaeosauridae

WHEN IT LIVED: Late Cretaceous

WHERE IT LIVED: Montana

SIZE: 9 feet long, 175 pounds

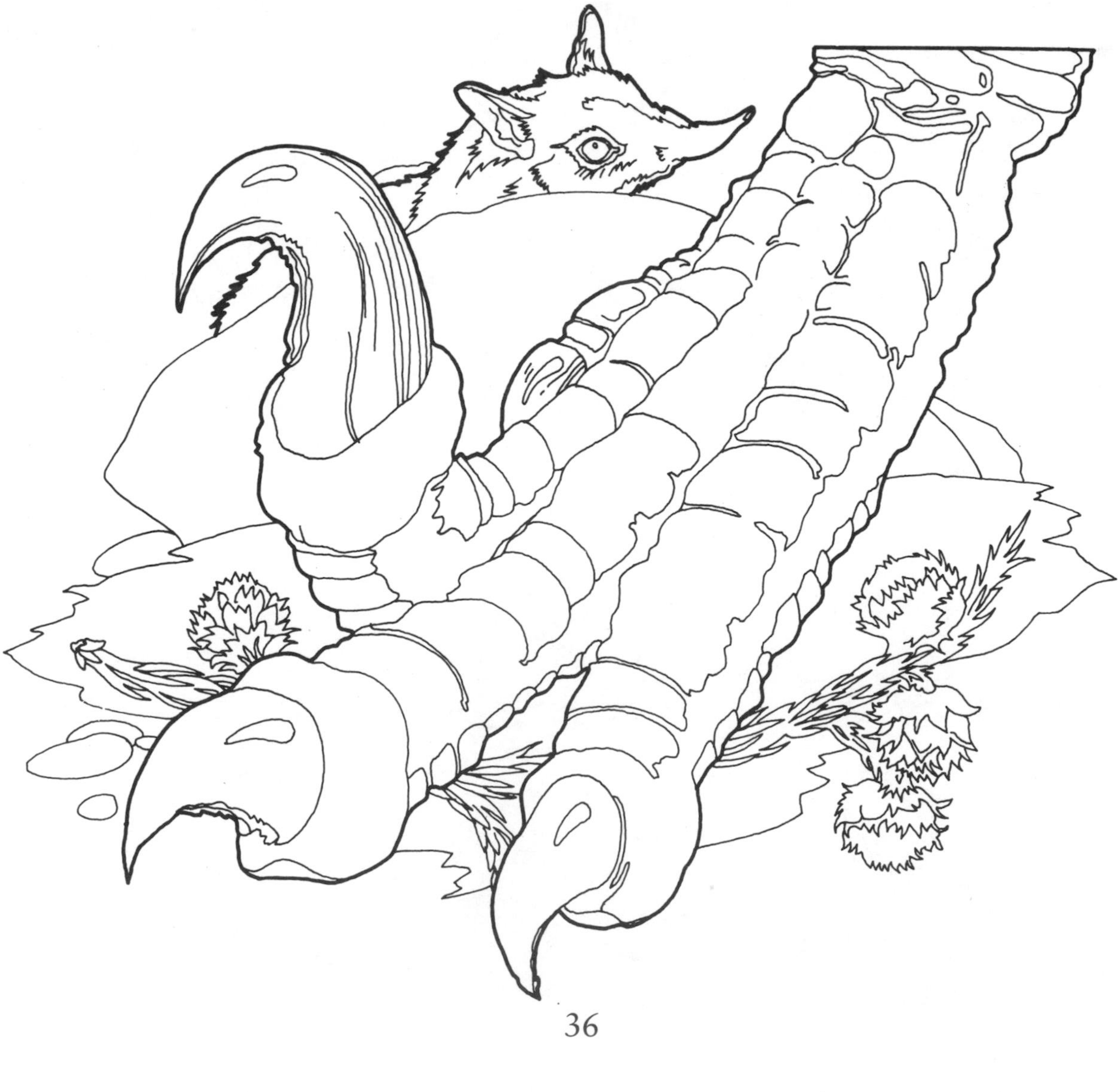

Egg Robbers

The "egg thief lizards," or *Oviraptorosauria*, were small dinosaurs. They had short jaws, parrot-like beaks, and no teeth. Their front limbs were long, and each hand had three fingers with sharp, curved claws. But from the size of their braincases, we know that their brains were comparatively large for dinosaurs, who had notoriously small brains.

Dino Facts

NAME: *Oviraptor* ("egg thief")
GROUP: Oviraptorosauria
WHEN IT LIVED: Late Cretaceous
WHERE IT LIVED: Mongolia
SIZE: 5 feet long

Most likely, Oviraptorosaurs were not hunters. Unlike most theropods, oviraptorans may have stolen and eaten eggs, insects, and plants. They also may have scavenged flesh from dead animals.

Their skulls were small and light, but their jaws were extremely strong and worked like powerful hedge clippers. These jaws were ideal for cutting through the tough leaves and other vegetation that grew when these dinosaurs lived.

The first fossil bones of *Oviraptor* were discovered in Mongolia during the 1920s, near a nest of dinosaur eggs. Because these eggs were thought to be those of the horned dinosaur *Protoceratops*, it was assumed that *Oviraptor* was stealing these eggs when it died. It is now believed that these eggs belonged to *Oviraptor* itself—so perhaps this *Oviraptor* perished while guarding its *own* eggs.

Many *Oviraptor* specimens have since been found. Some *Oviraptor* skulls feature large crests, which were probably used for displays, like the crests of other dinosaurs. But because of these crests, it is sometimes difficult, upon first glance, to tell the front part of an *Oviraptor's* head from the back.

Foot Lizards

The "foot lizards," or *Elmisauridae*, are a group of coelurosaurs that are closely related to oviraptors.

Elmisaurus, the dinosaur after which this group was named, was a small, lightly-built theropod. It had delicate hands and large feet—its most striking feature. *Elmisaurus's* foot bones are tightly fused together into a single unit—a feature previously known only in birds. Little else is known about how this coelurosaur looked, but for the purposes of this book, we have illustrated one possible example.

Chirostenotes, another possible "foot lizard," had long hind legs and big feet that could have been for wading in water. It probably had a small tail, although we don't know this for certain.

Dino Facts

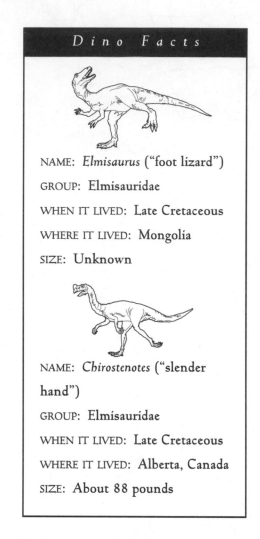

NAME: *Elmisaurus* ("foot lizard")
GROUP: Elmisauridae
WHEN IT LIVED: Late Cretaceous
WHERE IT LIVED: Mongolia
SIZE: Unknown

NAME: *Chirostenotes* ("slender hand")
GROUP: Elmisauridae
WHEN IT LIVED: Late Cretaceous
WHERE IT LIVED: Alberta, Canada
SIZE: About 88 pounds

Its hands were well suited for collecting mollusks, other animals without backbones, and eggs. On each hand its long and slender third fingers could be used to pry insects and other invertebrates from crevices in trees or streams. They may also have used this finger for grooming—these animals may have cleaned their scales the way birds today clean their feathers.

In the early 1930s, when this dinosaur was discovered, it was known only from a left and right hand. Each hand had three fingers, and its second finger was especially long. Now *Chirostenotes* is known from other specimens, including an incomplete skeleton.

Tyrant Lizards

The most famous meat-eating dinosaur—and one of the best known dinosaurs of all—is *Tyrannosaurus*. This giant is the basis for an entire group of very large coelurosaurs called *Tyrannosauridae*.

Tyrannosaurids were massive animals. They had very large heads and rough, lumpy snouts. Their necks, torsos, and forelimbs were extremely short, and their hands had only two functional fingers.

Tyrannosaurus itself was among the most powerful creatures ever to stalk this planet. Its head was more than 4 feet long, and its huge mouth was lined with serrated teeth the size of steak knives. Though its forelimbs were less than 3 feet long, each limb could lift about 450 pounds!

Dino Facts

NAME: *Tyrannosaurus* ("tyrant lizard")

GROUP: Tyrannosauridae

WHEN IT LIVED: Late Cretaceous

WHERE IT LIVED: Montana, South Dakota, New Mexico, Wyoming, Texas; Alberta, Saskatchewan, Canada; Mongolia; China

SIZE: 40 feet long, 6 tons

Some paleontologists believe that *Tyrannosaurus* was an active hunter, able to run nearly 40 miles per hour. Others, however, believe that this

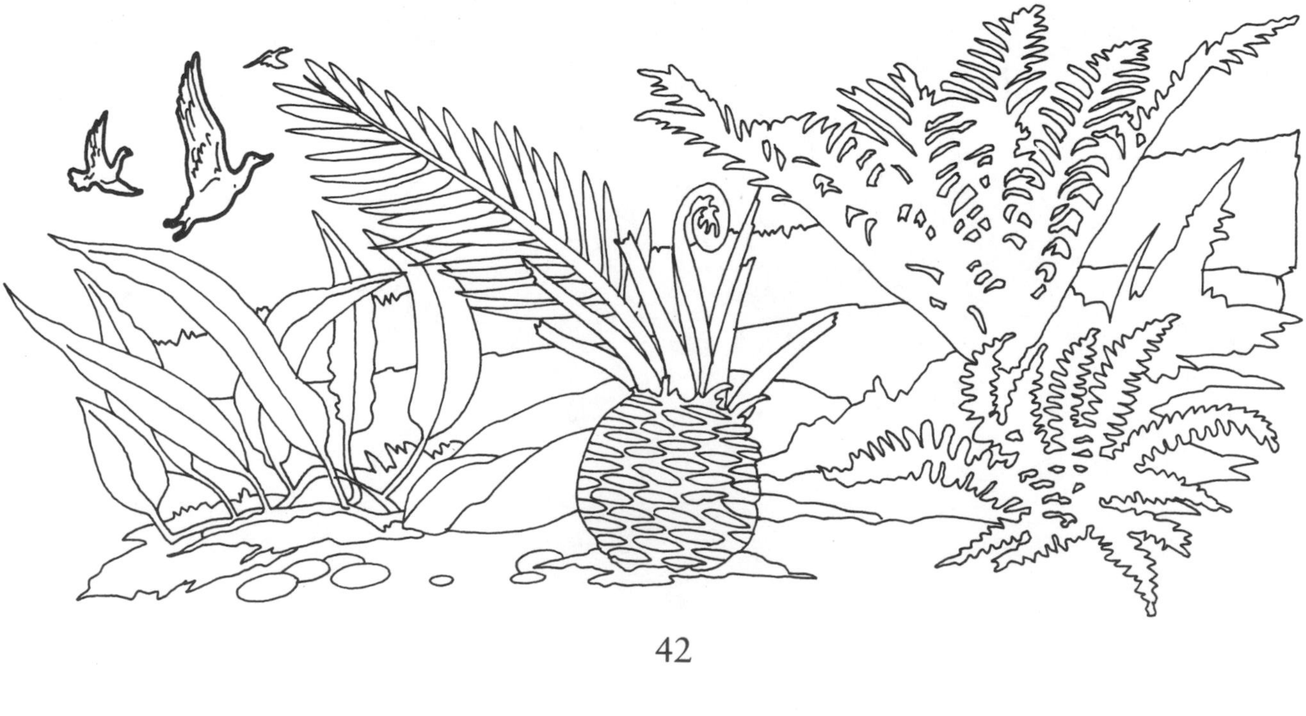

massive animal was really a scavenger, feeding off already dead animals. Still others suggest that it was both, hunting when it was younger and smaller, scavenging when it grew older and larger. Whichever theory is closest to the truth, *Tyrannosaurus* was a powerful killing machine.

Albertosaurus, another tyrannosaurid, had a narrow head, with one eye on each side. Half the weight of *Tyrannosaurus* and about ¾ the length, the smaller and sleeker *Albertosaurus* was probably swifter and more agile. This means that it hunted faster prey.

In 1988, the unusual tyrannosaurid *Nanotyrannus* was named. Apparently a pygmy, this dinosaur's skull is only 22 inches long. Unlike *Albertosaurus,* its eyes were directed forward to allow for stereo vision and better depth perception. Paper-thin sheets of bone in its inner snout wall suggest that it had an acute sense of smell, like dogs.

Nanotyranus's inner ear bones were surrounded by air chambers used to increase hearing sensitivity to low-frequency sounds, and its cheekbones had grooves, indicating that its ears pointed forward for stereo hearing. Small teeth indicate that it had a delicate bite, suitable for attacking small animals weighing no more than 60 pounds. This meant that *Nanotyrannus* could coexist with larger tyrannosaurids without competing against them for food.

Dino Facts

NAME: *Albertosaurus* ("Alberta lizard")

GROUP: Tyrannosauridae

WHEN IT LIVED: Late Cretaceous

WHERE IT LIVED: Alberta, Canada; Montana, Wyoming, New Mexico

SIZE: 30 feet long, 3 tons

NAME: *Nanotyrannus* ("dwarf tyrant")

GROUP: Tyrannosauridae

WHEN IT LIVED: Late Cretaceous

WHERE IT LIVED: Montana

SIZE: Length unknown, 600 to 1,000 pounds

Wound Tooths

The Troodontidae, or "wound tooths," were named for their dangerous serrated teeth.

Troodontids were rather small, lightly-built, Late Cretaceous coelurosaurians. But they were probably the smartest of all dinosaurs—their long and narrow heads held the largest dinosaurian brains (relative to body size).

Troodon, the dinosaur that gave this group its name, had a brain that weighed between 377 and 484 ounces, a long neck that was one-fourth its body length, long forelimbs slightly shorter than its neck, and long, flexible fingers that were about ¼ as long as the entire forelimb. The large claw of its second toe, similar to the "killer claw" of dromaeosaurids, made a dangerous offensive weapon.

Dino Facts

NAME: *Troodon* ("wound tooth")

GROUP: Troodontidae

WHEN IT LIVED: Late Cretaceous

WHERE IT LIVED: Alberta, Canada; Montana, Wyoming

SIZE: 6 feet long

Troodon's large saucer-like eyes faced forward. They were not set on the sides of the head as were the eyes of most dinosaurs. This gave *Troodon* good vision and let the animal see in three dimensions.

Because of its large brain, *Troodon* is regarded by some paleontologists as the smartest of all known dinosaurs. However, this does not mean that troodontids were *smart.* On an IQ level, troodontids were probably as smart as today's large flightless ground birds, like the emu. (An emu is *not* very smart. It cannot even be trained to walk or run in a particular direction.)

The "smartness" of a troodontid was most likely related to basic behavior such as reflexes and limb control, not to any kind of reasoning. (For example, *no* dinosaur was intelligent enough to open a door. They *might* have been smart enough to go *through* an already opened door, however.)

Troodontids were real terrors of the night. They probably hunted mammals, lizards, and other small animals when it was too dark for other theropods to see well. Moving swiftly and nimbly, they could catch their unsuspecting prey with their long grasping hands.

Ostrich Mimics

The "bird mimic lizards," Ornithomimosauria, were commonly known as "ostrich dinosaurs." But they were not related to these ground-dwelling birds, though they may have looked like dinosaurian versions of them.

Most ornithomimosaurs were medium-sized dinosaurs, 12 to 15 feet long. Their heads were delicate, with thin skull bones—they were not massive like the larger theropods. They had long snouts, beak-like jaws covered with horny material, and big eyes. Most were toothless, and all had long necks. Their forelimbs and hands were weak and probably of little use in acquiring food—so most likely, these dinosaurs ate not only meat, but also insects, eggs, and plants.

Most famous ornithomimosaurs were *Struthiomimus* and its slightly larger relative *Ornithomimus*. Largest of all known ornithomimosaurs was *Gallimimus*.

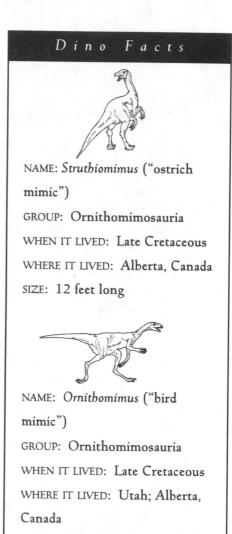

Dino Facts

NAME: *Struthiomimus* ("ostrich mimic")
GROUP: Ornithomimosauria
WHEN IT LIVED: Late Cretaceous
WHERE IT LIVED: Alberta, Canada
SIZE: 12 feet long

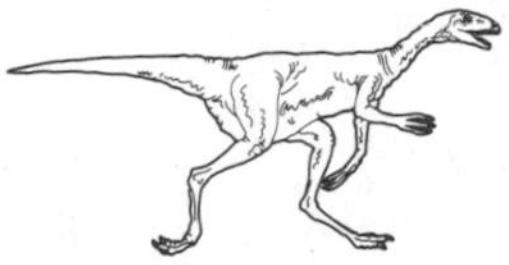

NAME: *Ornithomimus* ("bird mimic")
GROUP: Ornithomimosauria
WHEN IT LIVED: Late Cretaceous
WHERE IT LIVED: Utah; Alberta, Canada
SIZE: 15 feet long

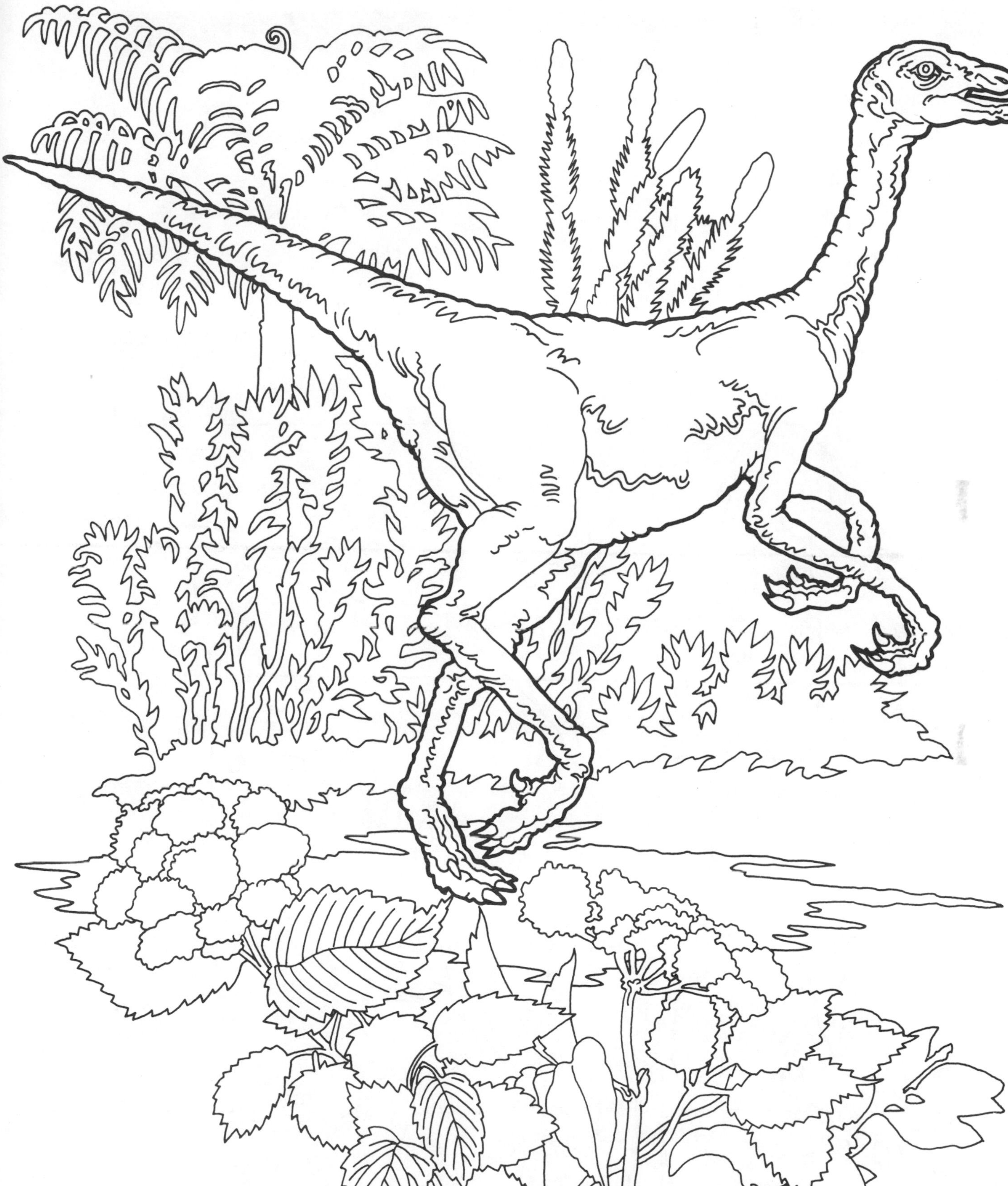

From their long legs and stiff tails, it is obvious that ornithomimosaurs were fast runners—the fastest, in fact, of all running dinosaurs. Their speed came in handy not only for capturing small prey but also for avoiding *becoming* the prey of larger meat-eating dinosaurs.

Dino Facts

NAME: *Gallimimus* ("rooster mimic")

GROUP: Ornithomimosauria

WHEN IT LIVED: Late Cretaceous

WHERE IT LIVED: Mongolia

SIZE: 20 feet long

Scythe Lizards

The science of paleontology has its surprises, and one such surprise was the discovery of a group of Late Cretaceous, saurischian dinosaurs commonly called the "scythe lizards," or Therizinosauridae.

Dino Facts

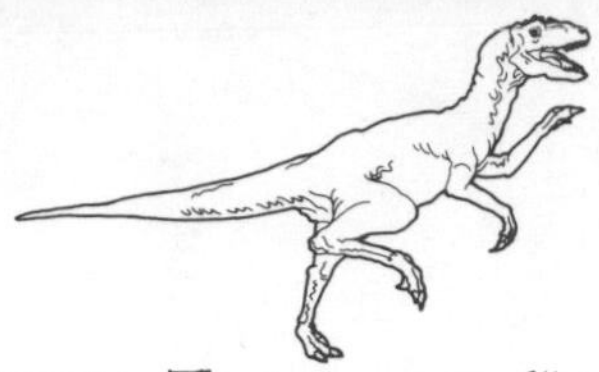

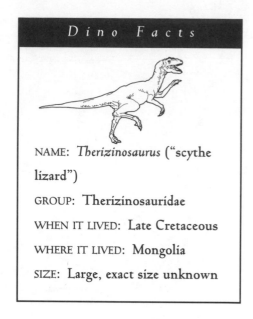

NAME: *Therizinosaurus* ("scythe lizard")

GROUP: Therizinosauridae

WHEN IT LIVED: Late Cretaceous

WHERE IT LIVED: Mongolia

SIZE: Large, exact size unknown

Named after *Therizinosaurus*, an animal whose fossil bones were first thought to be those of a giant turtle, paleontologists were long puzzled as to how to classify this dinosaur and its relatives. But later discoveries and studies of more fossil specimens have revealed that therizinosaurids are an unusual breed of theropods, possibly belonging to the group Coelurosauria.

Therizinosaurids had long front legs and strong, thick hindlimbs. Unlike most theropods, therizinosaurids had horn-covered beaks. Their mouths contained a toothless area, and then a series of cheek teeth—flat teeth in the back of the mouth, like our molars. This arrangement suggests that these were among the few kinds of theropods that ate plants instead of meat.

According to recent interpretations, which may or may not be correct, *Therizinosaurus* resembled a dinosaurian gorilla or sloth—paleontologists do not know for sure (the illustrations depict one possible example of its appearance). Its forearms were unusually large (8 feet long) and very strong, with extremely long fingers that had 2-foot long claws. Its tail was very short, perhaps too short to touch the ground. It probably fed by sitting down and then tearing off branches of trees, or pulling out shrubbery with its powerful hands and forelimbs.

Other Meat-Eaters

Some theropod dinosaurs do not fit into any particular group.

Known only from incomplete specimens, the unusual *Spinosaurus* seems to have been even larger than *Tyrannosaurus*. *Spinosaurus* was distinguished by the very long spines along its back. These spines probably supported a fleshy "sail" that may have served as a radiator to control the animal's body temperature, like the large ears of elephants.

Turning its sail toward the sun, *Spinosaurus* could take in heat to warm up. Turning it away from the sun, the animal could throw off heat to cool down. The sail may also have attracted females, if only males had it (or if males had a different sail than females did).

Baryonyx had a long, low "crocodile-like" snout with a spoon-shaped tip, long forelimbs, and very large foreclaws. *Baryonyx* was probably a fish-eater that waited on the shores of rivers to catch its meals. Because of similarities in bone structure, some paleontologists believe that *Baryonyx* and *Spinosaurus* were closely related.

Deinocheirus is known only from a pair

Dino Facts

NAME: *Spinosaurus* ("spiny lizard")
GROUP: Unknown
WHEN IT LIVED: Late Cretaceous
WHERE IT LIVED: Egypt
SIZE: About 50 feet long, 4.5 tons

NAME: *Baryonyx* ("heavy claw")
GROUP: Unknown
WHEN IT LIVED: Early Cretaceous
WHERE IT LIVED: England; Niger, Africa
SIZE: About 32 feet long, 1.8 tons

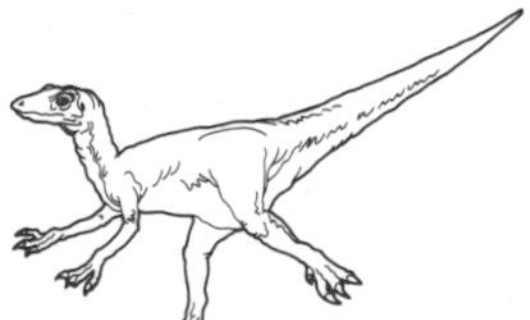

NAME: *Deinocheirus* ("terrible hand")
GROUP: Unknown
WHEN IT LIVED: Late Cretaceous
WHERE IT LIVED: Mongolia
SIZE: Very large, exact size unknown

of enormous forelimbs and hands. Its arms were 9 feet long, and its hands were 2 feet long, designed for grasping. Just what this animal looked like and how these hands were used are not known, but some scientists think that *Deinocheirus* used its huge hands to dig up anthills. Another theory is that *Deinocheirus* utilized its forelimbs to hang upside down from treelimbs!

Lizard-Footed Forms

The largest dinosaurs of all are the "lizard-footed forms" or *Sauropodomorpha*, one of the two major groups of "lizard-hipped" dinosaurs.

Sauropodomorphs had small, sometimes tiny heads and extremely long necks. Their bones were heavy, their hindlegs stocky, and front and back feet had five toes each. From the structure of their teeth, which were designed more for grinding than tearing, we know that sauropodomorphs ate only plants. These dinosaurs ranged in size from very small (such as the 8-foot-long *Anchisaurus*) to truly gigantic (like *Ultrasaurus,* more than 80 feet long).

Sauropodomorphs first appeared during the Late Triassic. They were around in one form or another until the Late Cretaceous. For much of the Mesozoic, sauropodomorphs were the dominant plant-eating land animals, their long necks allowing them to feed on many different kinds of vegetation—from the ground up to the tops of trees.

Dino Facts

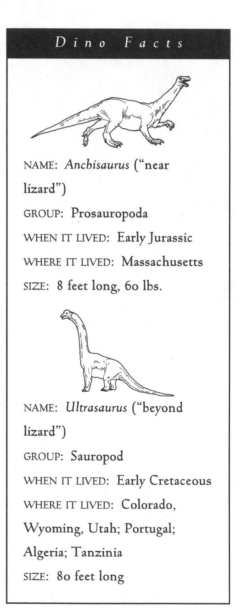

NAME: *Anchisaurus* ("near lizard")
GROUP: Prosauropoda
WHEN IT LIVED: Early Jurassic
WHERE IT LIVED: Massachusetts
SIZE: 8 feet long, 60 lbs.

NAME: *Ultrasaurus* ("beyond lizard")
GROUP: Sauropod
WHEN IT LIVED: Early Cretaceous
WHERE IT LIVED: Colorado, Wyoming, Utah; Portugal; Algeria; Tanzinia
SIZE: 80 feet long

Before the Sauropods

Members of the Prosauropoda ("before sauropods"), the more primitive sauropodomorph group that lived from the Late Triassic to Early Jurassic, were probably related to the later sauropods.

Until the arrival of this group of dinosaurs, all plant-eating land animals were squat creatures that could only eat vegetation growing on or close to the ground. So because of their long necks, prosauropods had an advantage over other plant-eating animals. They could eat plants that grew higher up, as well as those that grew at ground level. This helped the prosauropods to become the dominant plant eaters of their day.

Prosauropods ranged from small (such as *Anchisaurus*, 8 feet long) to large (*Plateosaurus*, 27 feet long). Some prosauropods walked on their hind legs, but most walked on all fours. Their heads were small, their teeth leaf-shaped, and their necks rather long.

Dino Facts

NAME: *Thecodontosaurus* ("socket-toothed lizard," because its teeth were set in tooth sockets)
GROUP: Prosauropoda
WHEN IT LIVED: Late Triassic
WHERE IT LIVED: England, Wales
SIZE: 10 feet long

NAME: *Plateosaurus* ("flat lizard," because of its flat teeth)
GROUP: Prosauropoda
WHEN IT LIVED: Late Triassic
WHERE IT LIVED: Germany, Switzerland, France
SIZE: 27 feet long

Thecodontosaurus was a preview of what was to come. Though small, lightly-built, and slender-limbed, this dinosaur had the basic body plan—the small head and long neck—of the later, larger prosauropods.

The first really big prosauropod was *Plateosaurus*. It walked on all fours,

but could probably rear up on its hind legs when it had to reach high-growing vegetation or to defend itself. *Plateosaurus* had a large hand claw that could rake foliage and could even be used as a weapon.

Lizard Feet

Sauropods, or "lizard feet," were the true giants of the Dinosauria. They were bigger than the biggest prosauropods. Some, like *Seismosaurus*, which was more than 100 feet long, were gigantic. But Sauropod heads were quite small, usually less than 2 feet long. And inside those tiny heads were the smallest brains of all dinosaurs, compared to body size. A sauropod brain could easily be held in one of your hands.

Sauropods walked on four strong pillar-like legs, and some may have been able to rear up on their hind legs. Their tails ranged from very short, as in *Brachiosaurus* whose tail was shorter than its neck, to very long, with the tail sometimes longer than the neck and rest of the body combined.

The earliest and most primitive known sauropod seems to be *Vulcanodon*, or "fire tooth," although some paleontologists believe this dinosaur was an advanced prosauropod. Very little is known about this dinosaur.

Dino Facts

NAME: *Vulcanodon* ("fire tooth," because its fossils were found between lava flows)
GROUP: Sauropoda
WHEN IT LIVED: Early Jurassic
WHERE IT LIVED: Zimbabwe, Africa
SIZE: 40 feet long

NAME: *Camarasaurus* ("chambered lizard," for openings in its vertebrae)
GROUP: Sauropoda
WHEN IT LIVED: Late Jurassic
WHERE IT LIVED: Utah, Wyoming, Montana, Colorado, New Mexico; Portugal
SIZE: 60 feet long, 25 tons

Camarasaurus was one of the most common sauropods. It had a boxlike head, legs that were all the same size, and a shorter and thicker neck than most other sauropods. Because the early specimens of this dinosaur were juveniles, *Camarasaurus* was once thought of as a rather small sauropod. Actually, adults grew to become quite large, more than 60 feet long.

All sauropods had the same general body shape, but scientists have discovered a few surprises over the years. *Saltasaurus*, for example, had numerous large bony plates imbedded in its hide. This armor may have helped to protect it from the teeth and claws of carnivorous dinosaurs.

Shunosaurus had a more direct way to discourage pesky meat-eaters. This sauropod sported a clubbed tail, and when it swung the tail, this club could inflict considerable damage on an attacker.

Dino Facts

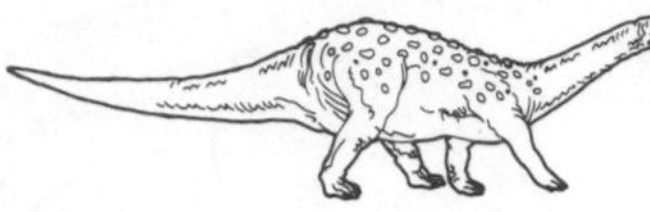

NAME: *Saltasaurus* ("Salta province lizard")
GROUP: Sauropoda
WHEN IT LIVED: Late Cretaceous
WHERE IT LIVED: Argentina, Uruguay
SIZE: Large, exact size unknown

NAME: *Shunosaurus* ("Sichuan lizard," after a part of China)
GROUP: Sauropoda
WHEN IT LIVED: Middle Jurassic
WHERE IT LIVED: China
SIZE: 40 feet long

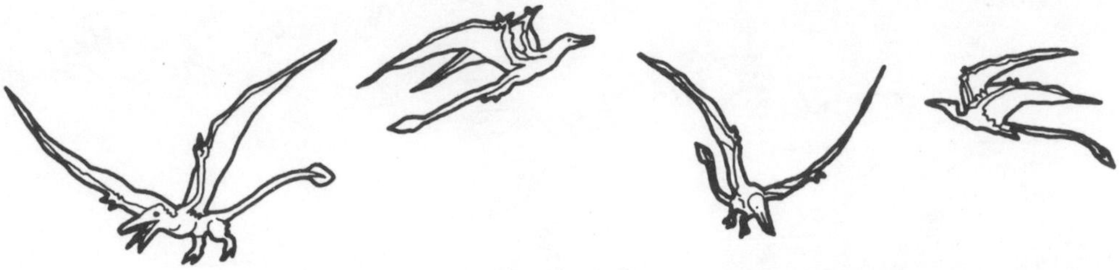

The Biggest of the Big

Once known as *Brontosaurus, Apatosaurus* is probably the most famous dinosaur of them all. This massive dinosaur and its longer, slender relative *Diplodocus* were two members of the sauropod subgroup Diplodocidae.

Diplodocids were gigantic and weighed 30 tons or more. Some were extremely long—reaching lengths of more than 100 feet! Their heads were elongated, not boxy, like *Camarasaurus*, with their nostrils on top of the nose, and with delicate teeth in the front of their mouths. Their tails were long and tapered, sometimes ending in a "whiplash." When snapped or cracked like a bullwhip, these tails served as weapons to fend off hungry theropods.

Bigger and heavier than *Apatosaurus* and *Diplodocus* was *Brachiosaurus*. *Brachiosaurus* had a very long neck, about as long as the rest of its body and tail combined. Its front legs were longer than its hind legs, so its back

Dino Facts

NAME: *Apatosaurus* ("deceptive lizard," because it was once confused with other sauropods)
GROUP: Diplodocidae
WHEN IT LIVED: Late Jurassic
WHERE IT LIVED: Colorado, Utah, Wyoming
SIZE: 75 feet long, 30 tons

NAME: *Diplodocus* ("double beam," for a feature of the tail vertebrae)
GROUP: Diplodocidae
WHEN IT LIVED: Late Jurassic-Early Cretaceous
WHERE IT LIVED: Colorado, Wyoming, Utah
SIZE: 90 feet long, 25 tons

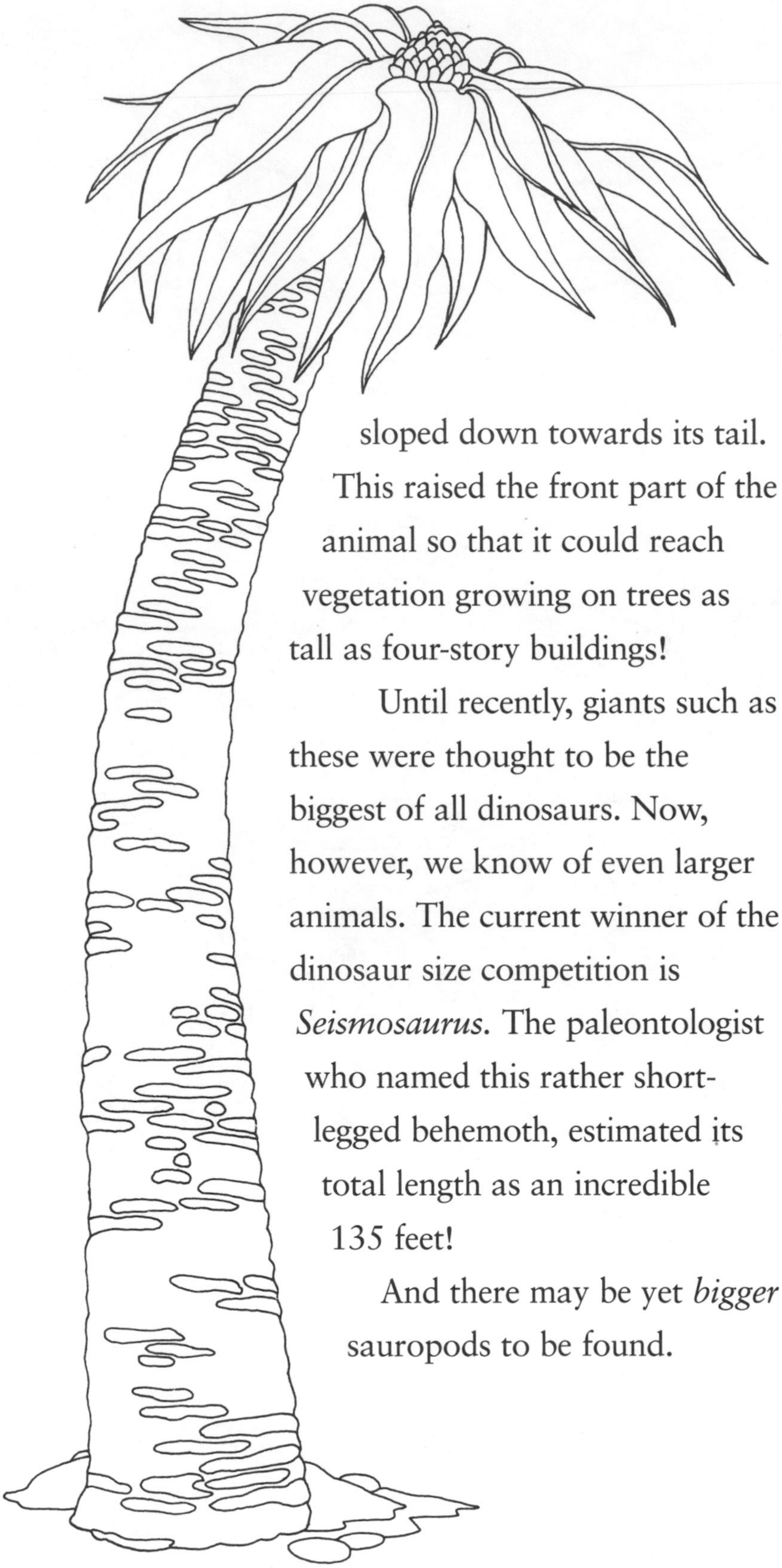

sloped down towards its tail. This raised the front part of the animal so that it could reach vegetation growing on trees as tall as four-story buildings!

Until recently, giants such as these were thought to be the biggest of all dinosaurs. Now, however, we know of even larger animals. The current winner of the dinosaur size competition is *Seismosaurus*. The paleontologist who named this rather short-legged behemoth, estimated its total length as an incredible 135 feet!

And there may be yet *bigger* sauropods to be found.

Dino Facts

NAME: ***Brachiosaurus*** **("arm lizard," for its long forearms)**

GROUP: **Brachiosauridae**

WHEN IT LIVED: **Late Jurassic–Early Cretaceous**

WHERE IT LIVED: **Colorado, Utah, Wyoming; Tanzania, Algeria, Africa; Portugal**

SIZE: **80 feet long, at least 40 tons**

NAME: ***Seismosaurus*** **("earth shaker lizard")**

GROUP: **Diplodocidae**

WHEN IT LIVED: **Late Jurassic**

WHERE IT LIVED: **New Mexico**

SIZE: **At least 100 feet long**

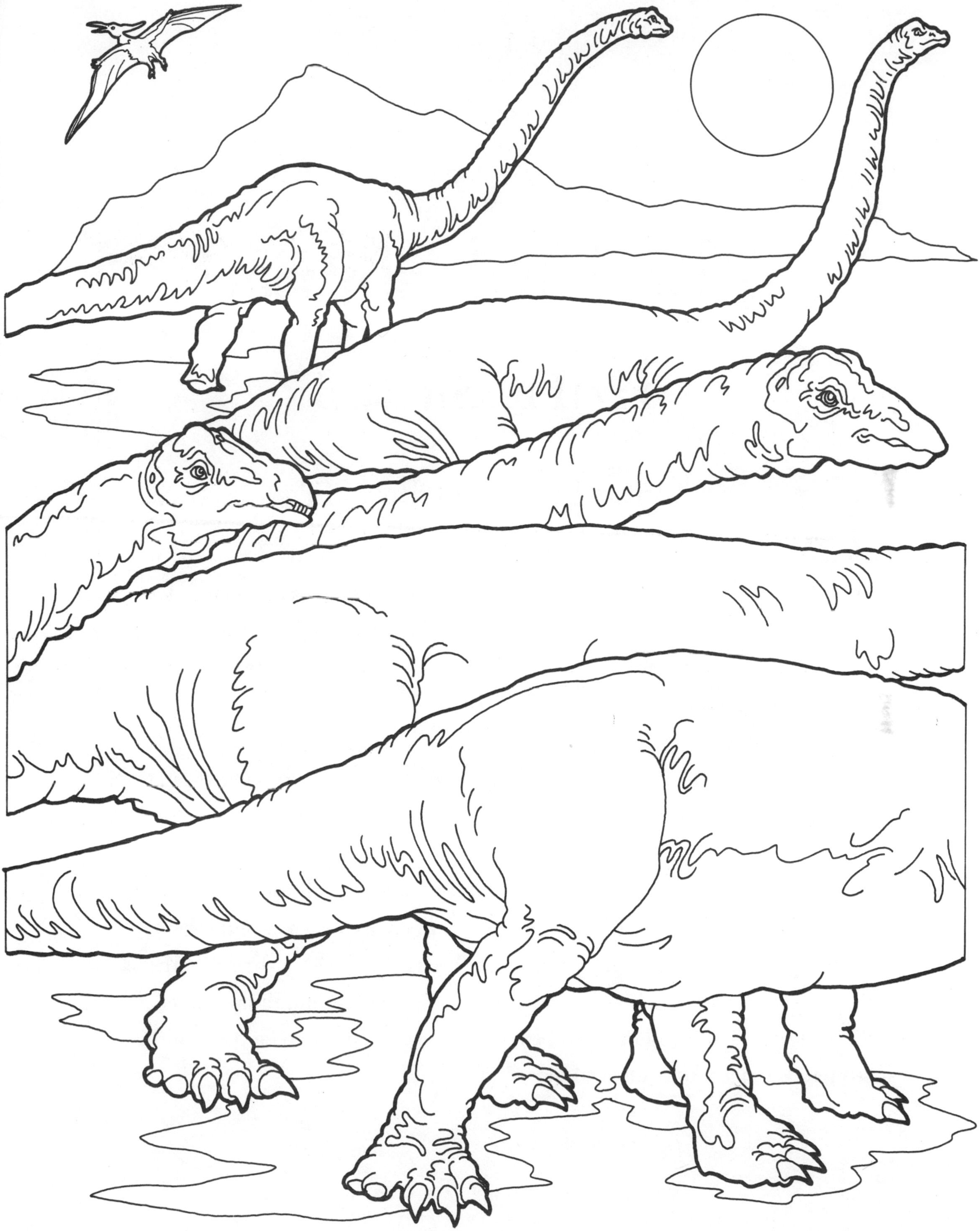

PART THREE:

The Bird-Hipped Dinosaurs

Ornithischia: The Bird Hips

Despite their name, the Ornithischia, or "bird-hipped" dinosaurs, were a large and diverse group that were even *less* birdlike than saurischians. The Ornithischia were named for the bones of their pelvises which were arranged like those of modern birds. This group apparently branched off from the Saurischia sometime during the Late Triassic.

All ornithischians had a horn-covered beak-like bone called a "predentary" at the front of the mouth, a useful tool for cropping vegetation. Ornithischians were herbivorous, and they ranged in size from the 4-foot long armored dinosaur *Scutellosaurus* to the 40-foot long duck-billed dinosaur *Saurolophus*. Some walked on their hind legs, some on all fours, some both.

Most had flat cheek teeth at the sides and back of their mouths for chewing vegetation, and their pouchlike cheeks held food in their mouths as they chewed. Ornithischians also had bigger stomachs than saurischians. These features allowed them to better chew plants and to keep them in their stomachs longer for improved digestion.

DINOSAUR HIP BONES

There was a lot of variety among ornithischians, more so than among the lizard-hipped dinosaurs. Some ornithischians sported flashy head crests, horns, or other ornamentation. Some of them had body armor, like plates and scutes.

The ornithischians were among the last dinosaurs to die out.

Early "Bird-Hips"

Two small dinosaurs, each of them less than 7 feet long, were among the earliest known bird-hipped dinosaurs. Both of these dinosaurs probably looked fairly similar to each other.

The most primitive known ornithischian, *Pisanosaurus* was identified from a very incomplete skeleton, so we don't know much about this animal. We do know that it was only about 3 feet long, was lightly built, and had long and slender legs—signs of a good runner. *Pisanosaurus* was very primitive—so primitive, in fact, that some paleontologists once doubted that it was an ornithischian.

Many incomplete specimens of another bird-hipped dinosaur, *Lesothosaurus* have been found. This animal had short but fairly strong forelimbs. It probably walked on its hind legs, but came down on all fours to eat. Unlike later ornithischians, *Lesothosaurus* had no cheek teeth, which meant that since it had no cheeks to contain its food, it lost a lot of its dinner. Able to run very fast, *Lesothosaurus* probably spent much of its time fleeing from hungry meat-eaters.

Dino Facts

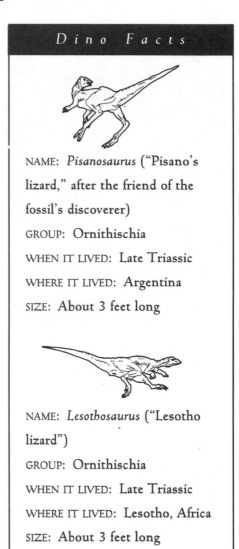

NAME: *Pisanosaurus* ("Pisano's lizard," after the friend of the fossil's discoverer)
GROUP: Ornithischia
WHEN IT LIVED: Late Triassic
WHERE IT LIVED: Argentina
SIZE: About 3 feet long

NAME: *Lesothosaurus* ("Lesotho lizard")
GROUP: Ornithischia
WHEN IT LIVED: Late Triassic
WHERE IT LIVED: Lesotho, Africa
SIZE: About 3 feet long

Shield Bearers

The "shield bearers," Thyreophora, were a very primitive ornithischian group, distinguished by their body armor—scutes, plates, and spikes.

The most primitive thyreophoran was *Emausaurus*. This dinosaur's armor was not as developed as the armor of later, more advanced thyreophorans. It was made up of small pieces of bone called osteoderms, which were shaped like cones or plates. *Emausaurus* was small, so it needed the armor to protect itself from larger meat-eaters that attacked.

Scutellosaurus was bigger than *Emausaurus*, and its armor was more elaborate. On the outside, *Scutellosaurus* resembled its larger relative *Scelidosaurus*. Both dinosaurs boasted rows of small bony plates and scutes along the neck, back, and tail.

But *Scelidosaurus* was more heavily armored than *Scutellosaurus* although the latter had another advantage. Being smaller and lighter, *Scuttelosaurus* could get up on its hind legs and run away quickly from a dangerous situation. The bigger, heavier *Scelidosaurus* had a much more difficult time escaping on all fours.

Dino Facts

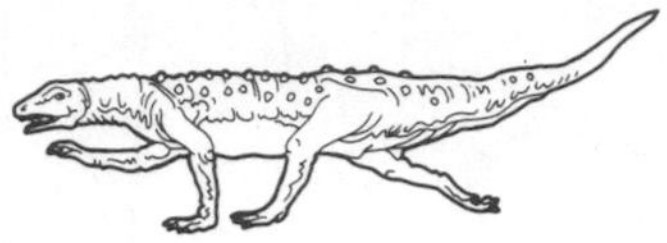

NAME: *Emausaurus* ("Ernst-Moritz-Arndt-Universität lizard")
GROUP: Thyreophora
WHEN IT LIVED: Early Jurassic
WHERE IT LIVED: Germany
SIZE: 7 feet long

NAME: *Scutellosaurus* ("bony plate lizard")
GROUP: Thyreophora
WHEN IT LIVED: Early Jurassic
WHERE IT LIVED: New Mexico, Arizona
SIZE: 4 feet long

NAME: *Scelidosaurus* ("ribbed lizard," because many ribs were found among its fossil remains)
GROUP: Thyreophora
WHEN IT LIVED: Early Jurassic
WHERE IT LIVED: England, Arizona
SIZE: 12 feet long

Roofed Lizards

The "roofed lizards," or Stegosauria, are easily identified by the two rows of plates and spikes that adorned their necks, backs, and tails. Some stegosaurs, like *Kentrosaurus* and *Tuojiangosaurus*, also had large spikes on their shoulders.

The earliest known stegosaur was *Huajangosaurus*. This dinosaur had two rows of small plates along its neck and back shaped like lances, and four tail spines. It also had teeth in the front of its mouth, a primitive feature not present in advanced stegosaurs.

The best-known and largest stegosaur is, of course, *Stegosaurus* itself. This dinosaur wore two rows of skin plates, some 2 feet high and 2 feet wide, and four tail spikes that faced backwards.

A stegosaur's tail spikes were formidable weapons. A stegosaur could swing its tail with enough force to fatally wound any theropod foolish enough to pursue it for dinner. Many an *Allosaurus* must have been painfully discouraged from its meal after being cut by the tail spikes of a *Stegosaurus*.

The function of the stegosaur's body plates,

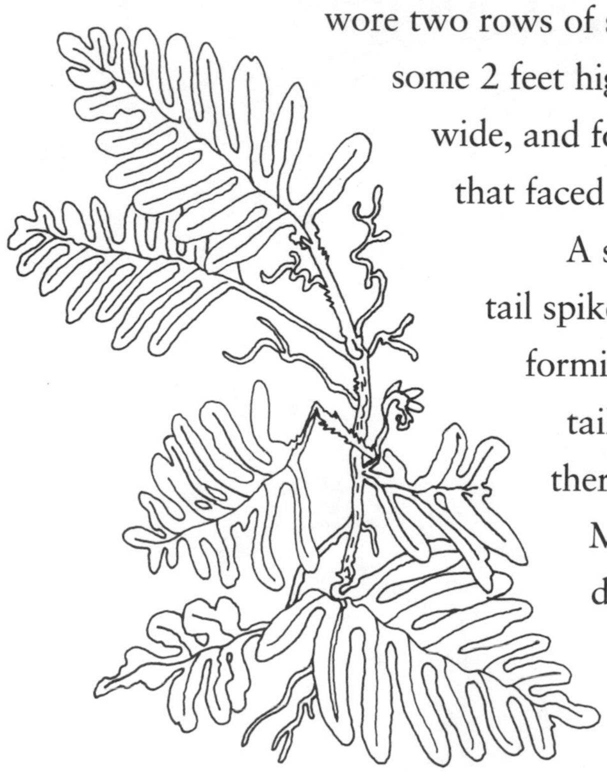

Dino Facts

NAME: *Kentrosaurus* ("spiked lizard")
GROUP: Stegosauria
WHEN IT LIVED: Late Jurassic
WHERE IT LIVED: Tanzania, Africa
SIZE: 16 feet long, 2 tons

NAME: *Huajangosaurus* ("Huayang, China, lizard")
GROUP: Stegosauria
WHEN IT LIVED: Middle Jurassic
WHERE IT LIVED: China
SIZE: 13.5 feet long

however, has long puzzled scientists. At one time the plates were thought to be defensive armor, but they would have left most of the animal's hide unprotected. Now it is believed that the plates served more than one function. First, they made the animal look taller in profile, helpful for scaring off predators. Without the plates on along the neck, back, and tail, the animal would have looked much smaller.

The plates may also have been very colorful and used to attract mates, just as the feathers of peacocks are used to attract peahens. And, like the back sail of *Spinosaurus*, a stegosaur's plates may have worked like solar panels to take in heat from the sun to warm its body.

Dino Facts

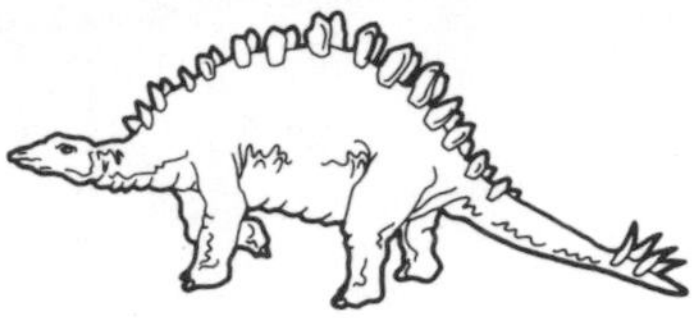

NAME: *Tuojiangosaurus* ("Tuojiang, China, lizard")
GROUP: Stegosauria
WHEN IT LIVED: Late Jurassic
WHERE IT LIVED: China
SIZE: 23.5 feet long

NAME: *Stegosaurus* ("roofed lizard")
GROUP: Stegosauria
WHEN IT LIVED: Late Jurassic(?)–Early Cretaceous
WHERE IT LIVED: Colorado, Wyoming, Utah
SIZE: 25 feet long

Fused Lizards

Members of the thyreophoran group Ankylosauria, or "fused lizards," were like living armored tanks.

Ankylosaurs were stocky and walked on all fours. Their armored heads were wide, covered by a mosaic of bony plates, and they carried them low. Their long tails took up about half their body length.

Their most distinctive feature was their body armor, made up of small rounded plates arranged in parallel strips. These bands formed a continuous bony shield on their backs for protection.

Ankylosaurs lived on every continent. They thrived in the Late Cretaceous, but early forms have been found in Upper Jurassic rocks. They were among the last groups of dinosaurs to die out. Their success rate was probably helped a great deal by their heavily armored bodies—about the only way a meat-eater could harm an ankylosaur was to turn it on its back so that its unprotected belly was exposed.

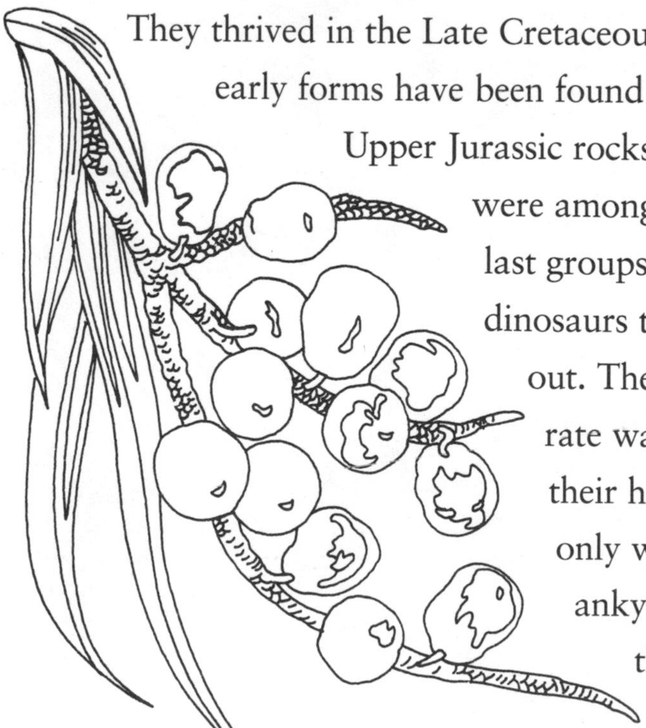

Dino Facts

NAME: *Nodosaurus* ("toothless lizard")
GROUP: Nodosauridae
WHEN IT LIVED: Late Cretaceous
WHERE IT LIVED: Wyoming, Kansas
SIZE: 17.5 feet

NAME: *Panoplosaurus* ("armored lizard")
GROUP: Nodosauridae
WHEN IT LIVED: Late Cretaceous
WHERE IT LIVED: Alberta, Canada
SIZE: 18 feet long, 3 tons

There were two ankylosaurian groups. Members of the more primitive "nodular lizards," Nodosauridae, had more upright bodies. Their heads were relatively long and pear-shaped, with bony plates, no horns, and small teeth. The sides of their bodies sometimes bore large spikes. Typical nodosaurids were *Nodosaurus* and *Panoplosaurus*.

More advanced ankylosaurs belonged to the group Ankylosauridae. These dinosaurs, such as *Ankylosaurus* and *Euoplocephalus*, had more robust bodies than nodosaurids. Their heads were triangular and bore prominent horns. Sometimes their bodies were lined with long spikes. An ankylosaurid also carried a powerful weapon—a heavy club of bone at the end of its tail. When swung, an *Ankylosaurus* tail club was just high enough to seriously wound the ankles of even the biggest meat-eating dinosaurs of the day.

Dino Facts

NAME: *Ankylosaurus* ("fused lizard," for its stiffened armor)
GROUP: Ankylosauria
WHEN IT LIVED: Late Cretaceous
WHERE IT LIVED: Wyoming, Montana; Alberta, Canada
SIZE: 25 feet long, 5 tons

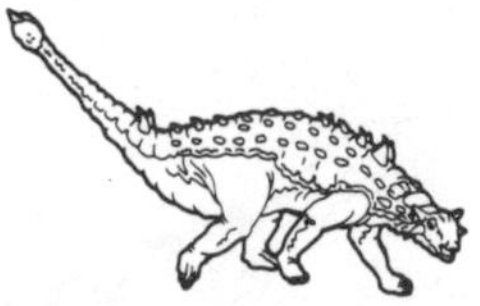

NAME: *Euoplocephalus* ("well-protected head")
GROUP: Ankylosauria
WHEN IT LIVED: Late Cretaceous
WHERE IT LIVED: Montana; Alberta, Canada
SIZE: 20 feet long, 3.5 tons

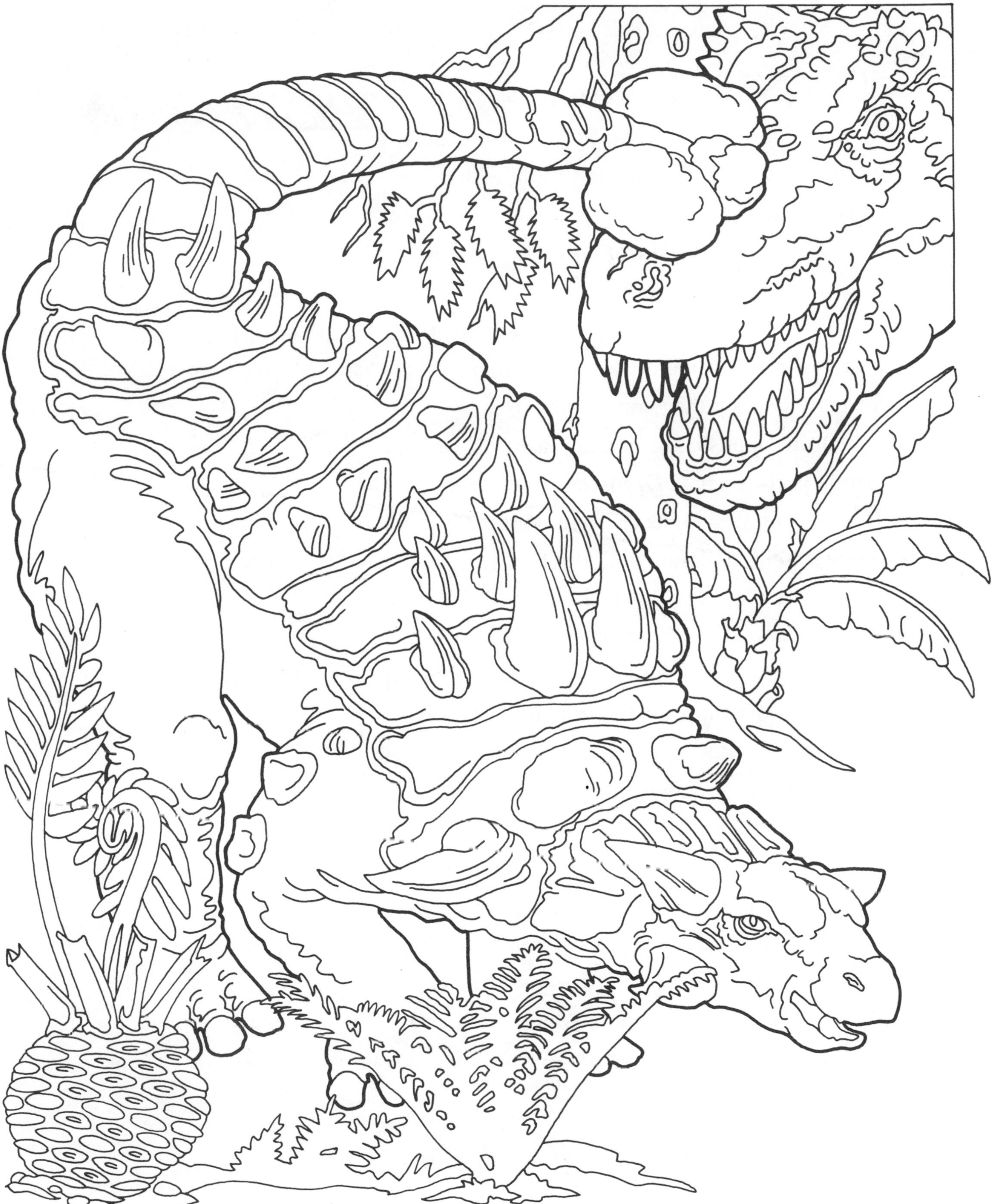

Bird Feet

The Ornithopoda, or "bird feet," were an advanced group of bird-hipped dinosaurs. In reality their feet were even less birdlike than those of theropods.

Ornithopods lived from the Late Triassic until almost the end of the Cretaceous. By then, they had become the world's dominant group of plant-eating dinosaurs, an honor formerly held by the giant sauropods.

Ornithopods came in many sizes. Small ornithopods, such as *Dryosaurus*, which was 12 feet long, were agile creatures that walked on their hind legs and could run fast. Large ornithopods, such as the duck-billed *Edmontosaurus,* could walk on two or four legs. All known ornithopods had horny beaks, which were useful for eating tough vegetation.

Dino Facts

NAME: *Heterodontosaurus* ("mixed-tooth lizard," because of its different kinds of teeth)
GROUP: Heterodontosauridae
WHEN IT LIVED: Late Triassic
WHERE IT LIVED: South Africa
SIZE: About 3 feet long

NAME: *Hypsilophodon* ("high-ridged tooth")
GROUP: Hypsilophodontidae
WHEN IT LIVED: Early Jurassic
WHERE IT LIVED: England, Spain
SIZE: 5 feet long, 140 pounds

The "mixed tooth lizards," Heterodontosauridae, included the smallest and earliest ornithischians. The best-known heterodontosaurid was the dinosaur after which the group was named, *Heterodontosaurus*—a lightly-built animal about the size of a turkey.

Heterodontosaurus had two long tusk-like teeth, in addition to many smaller teeth. Such teeth appear in meat-eating animals, but *Heterodontosaurus's* teeth may have acted as defensive weapons, like the oversized teeth of wild pigs today. They may also have been used for digging,

or for cutting food. Some scientists believe that only *Heterodontosaurus* males had these tusks and used them to establish their dominance over other males and to attract females.

The Hypsilophodontidae ("high-ridged teeth") resembled heterodontosaurids but were more advanced. Hypsilophodontids had strong jaws and teeth that overlapped to form a long cutting blade. Hypsilophodontids could eat more types of food than heterodontosaurids, including tougher vegetation, and this gave them an advantage over more primitive ornithopods.

The best known hypsilophodontid was *Hypsilophodon*. Because its long fingers and toes were originally thought to have been used to grasp branches, scientists once believed that *Hypsilophodon* spent much of its time in trees. Recent studies, however, have disproved this old notion. Today, we know *Hypsilophodon* was a fast-moving, ground-dwelling dinosaur, whose long, stiff tail made an ideal stabilizer when it ran.

Orodromeus was a very graceful animal. In addition, fossilized *Orodromeus* eggs show embryos with very well-developed bones, which indicated that *Orodromeus* hatchlings could fend for themselves and did not require parental care.

Dino Facts

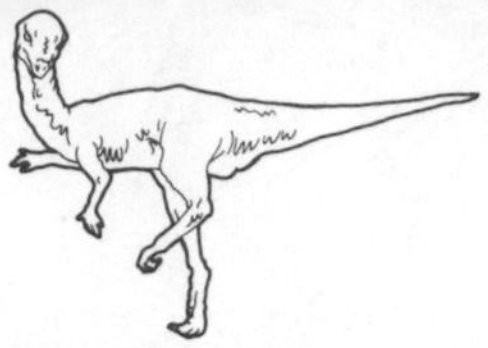

NAME: *Orodromeus* ("mountain runner")
GROUP: Hypsilophodontidae
WHEN IT LIVED: Late Cretaceous
WHERE IT LIVED: Montana
SIZE: Small, exact length unknown

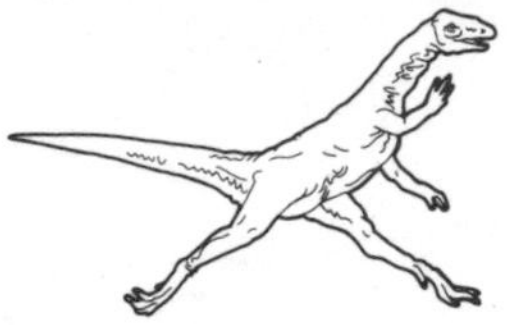

NAME: *Dryosaurus* ("oak lizard," for teeth shaped somewhat like oak leaves)
GROUP: Dryosauridae
WHEN IT LIVED: Late Jurassic
WHERE IT LIVED: Colorado, Wyoming, Utah; Tanzania, Africa
SIZE: 12 feet long, 170 pounds

Dryosaurus, the namesake of the group Dryosauridae, or "oak lizards," was similar to *Hypsilophodon*—but unlike *Hypsilophodon, Dryosaurus* did not have teeth in the front of its upper jaw.

Iguana Teeth

The Iguanodontidae, or "iguana teeth," had heads with long snouts, horny beaks for cropping food, and long jaws filled with numerous grinding teeth. Bigger than more primitive ornithopods, iguanodontids were well suited to eat the large amounts of vegetation needed to support their size.

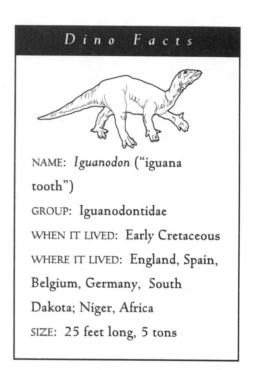

> **Dino Facts**
>
> 
>
> NAME: *Iguanodon* ("iguana tooth")
>
> GROUP: Iguanodontidae
>
> WHEN IT LIVED: Early Cretaceous
>
> WHERE IT LIVED: England, Spain, Belgium, Germany, South Dakota; Niger, Africa
>
> SIZE: 25 feet long, 5 tons

The shoulders and forelimbs of iguanodontids were large, and the second and third fingers of their huge hands were blunt and hoof-like and helped them to walk on all fours. They possessed large spiked thumbs, which they may have used as stabbing weapons. A hard jab of the thumb to another dinosaur's eye or to some other vulnerable spot would have discouraged any attack. This spike may also have been used as ornamentation to attract mates.

Iguanodon was the second dinosaur ever named. The first *Iguanodon* specimens found were fossil teeth discovered in the 1820s. They resembled large-scale versions of the teeth of modern-day iguanas. Fossil footprints attributed to *Iguanodon* show that it probably traveled in herds, like modern cattle.

Since *Iguanodon* was first described during the early days of dinosaur discoveries, many mistakes were made in describing how it looked. The earliest depictions of this dinosaur showed it walking on four elephant-like legs, and its thumb spike was misplaced as a nose horn.

Ouranosaurus was another large iguanodontid, distinguished by a prominent "sail" made up of skin stretched over very long back spines. As with the theropod *Spinosaurus*, the sail probably took in and gave off heat, allowing the animal some control over its body temperature.

Dino Facts

NAME: *Ouranosaurus* ("valiant lizard," after a native word to mean fearless animal)

GROUP: Iguanodontidae

WHEN IT LIVED: Early Cretaceous

WHERE IT LIVED: Niger

SIZE: 23 feet long

Big Lizards

The "big lizards," or Hadrosauridae, were the so-called "duck-billed" dinosaurs. These advanced ornithopods were not related to ducks, however—they were named for their flat, broad jaws which resembled ducks' bills.

Hadrosaurids are known from many specimens: some complete skeletons, fossilized skin samples, fossil "mummies," and even eggs. They were the last ornithopods to appear on Earth and were among the most diverse dinosaurs at the end of the Cretaceous, with their heads showing a wide range of variation.

These were large animals, with bodies similar to the iguanodontids (but without the spiked thumbs). Their fingers were covered in a fleshy "mitten," and both their fingers and toes were hooved. They walked on their hind legs and on all fours.

Telmatosaurus was the most primitive known hadrosaurid. Its relatively small size (16 feet long) suggests that this dinosaur was a dwarf hadrosaurid.

Dino Facts

NAME: *Telmatosaurus* ("marsh lizard," believed to inhabit marshes)
GROUP: Hadrosauridae
WHEN IT LIVED: Late Cretaceous
WHERE IT LIVED: Romania, France, Spain
SIZE: 16 feet long, 1100 pounds

NAME: *Edmontosaurus* ("Edmonton Formation lizard")
GROUP: Hadrosaurinae
WHEN IT LIVED: Late Cretaceous
WHERE IT LIVED: Alberta, Saskatchewan, Canada; North Dakota, South Dakota, Wyoming, Colorado
SIZE: 40 feet long, 4 tons

Members of the hadrosaurid subgroup Hadrosaurinae were more slender and graceful and had longer heads than members of the Lambeosaurinae ("Charles Lambe's lizards"). The heads of most hadrosaurines were also flat on top.

The best known hadrosaurine is *Edmontosaurus*—the classic duck-billed dinosaur. We know more about *Edmontosaurus* than many other kinds of dinosaurs, not only because of the number of skeletons paleontologists have found, but also thanks to the discovery of fossilized "mummies"—specimens in which the animal's skin and organs were preserved along with its bones.

In one well-preserved *Edmontosaurus* "mummy," the bones were still joined together and were covered with impressions of fossilized dehydrated skin. The hide was very thin and leathery, with a pebbly texture.

The largest known hadrosaurine was *Shantungosaurus*. This dinosaur was very much like *Edmontosaurus*, only bigger.

Dino Facts

NAME: *Shantungosaurus* ("Shantung, China lizard")
GROUP: Hadrosaurinae
WHEN IT LIVED: Late Cretaceous
WHERE IT LIVED: China
SIZE: 50 feet long

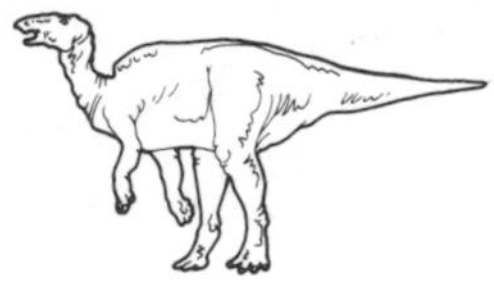

NAME: *Maiasaura* ("good mother lizard")
GROUP: Hadrosaurinae
WHEN IT LIVED: Late Cretaceous
WHERE IT LIVED: Montana
SIZE: 30 feet long

One of the most important dinosaur discoveries in recent years involved the hadrosaurine *Maiasaura*. In addition

to fossilized bones, paleontologists uncovered fossilized nests, eggs, embryos, hatchlings, and juveniles of this dinosaur. Until this discovery, dinosaurs were thought to have abandoned their eggs, like many modern reptiles do.

However, evidence shown by the *Maiasaura* fossils led paleontologist John R. Horner to believe that this dinosaur cared for its young in the nest, bringing them food and offering protection until they were old and large enough to take care of themselves! *Maiasaura* families also traveled together and were the first known dinosaur families.

Although most hadrosaurines had flat heads, some, like *Gryposaurus* and *Saurolophus*, sported solid crests of bone, the former on its nose and the latter at the back of its head. These crests may have helped the animals to tell each other apart and to attract mates.

Members of the Lambeosaurinae were larger and stronger than hadrosaurines. They had taller backs because of their long spines, and shorter front legs. But their most distinguishing feature was their head crests. These crests were hollow and were connected to the dinosaurs's nasal passages.

Dino Facts

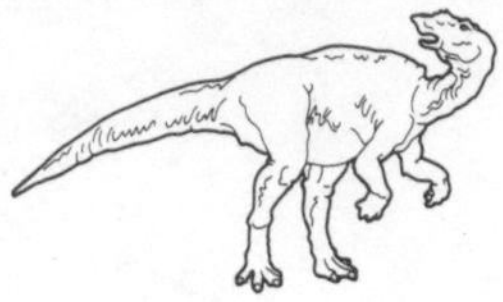

NAME: *Gryposaurus* ("Griffin lizard")
GROUP: Hadrosaurinae
WHEN IT LIVED: Late Cretaceous
WHERE IT LIVED: Montana
SIZE: 30 feet long, 3 tons

NAME: *Saurolophus* ("lizard crest")
GROUP: Hadrosaurinae
WHEN IT LIVED: Late Cretaceous
WHERE IT LIVED: Alberta, Canada; Mongolia, China
SIZE: 22-40 feet long

NAME: *Lambeosaurus* ("Charles Lambe's lizard," after the famous paleontologist)
GROUP: Lambeosaurinae
WHEN IT LIVED: Late Cretaceous
WHERE IT LIVED: Alberta, Canada; Baja, Mexico; New Mexico, Montana
SIZE: 40 feet long

Crest shapes varied among lambeosaurines. In *Lambeosaurus,* the crest resembled a hatchet with a backward-turned spike. In *Corythosaurus,* it looked like an ancient soldier's helmet. *Parasaurolophus's* crest was a 5-foot long tube that extended behind the animal's back and shoulders.

The purpose of these crests has long puzzled scientists. Duck-billed dinosaurs were once thought to have been mostly aquatic, and so the crests were then believed to be air-storage chambers for breathing underwater. Today, hadrosaurids are known to have lived on the land, so new theories have arisen. It is now believed that the crests enhanced the dinosaurs's sense of smell. They may also have functioned as resonance chambers for making sounds, possibly a call to warn others of danger.

Paleontologist David B. Weishampel performed experiments using a hollow tube to determine the purpose of the crests. He found that the long, tube-like crest of *Parasaurolophus* could make a sound like an old automobile horn!

Dino Facts

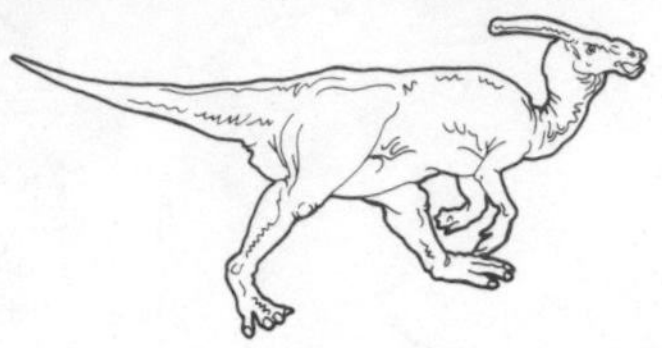

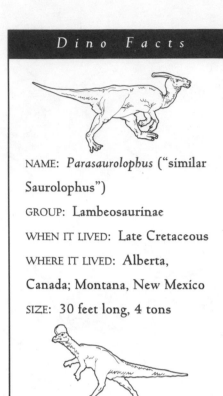

NAME: *Parasaurolophus* ("similar Saurolophus")

GROUP: Lambeosaurinae

WHEN IT LIVED: Late Cretaceous

WHERE IT LIVED: Alberta, Canada; Montana, New Mexico

SIZE: 30 feet long, 4 tons

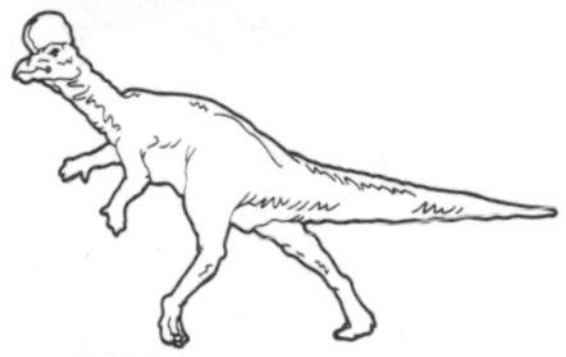

NAME: *Corythosaurus* ("helmet lizard")

GROUP: Lambeosaurinae

WHEN IT LIVED: Late Cretaceous

WHERE IT LIVED: Alberta, Canada; Montana

SIZE: 30 feet long, 3 tons

Thick-Headed Lizards

The "thick-headed lizards," or Pachycephalosauria, were also known as "bone-headed" dinosaurs. They were named for the top parts of their skull, which were as much as 9 inches thick! In some pachycephalosaurs, this thickening formed a dome of solid bone.

Most pachycephalosaurs lived during the Late Cretaceous, and all of them walked on their hind legs. Their faces were relatively short, their teeth small and leaflike. On their snouts and at the backs of their heads was ornamentation—various bony nodes and spikes.

The most primitive known pachycephalosaur was *Yaverlandia*. Its skullcap was so small it could rest on the palm of your hand. The biggest was *Pachycephalosaurus*. It had a massive, 9-inch–thick skull roof and a snout adorned with many bony nodes.

Dino Facts

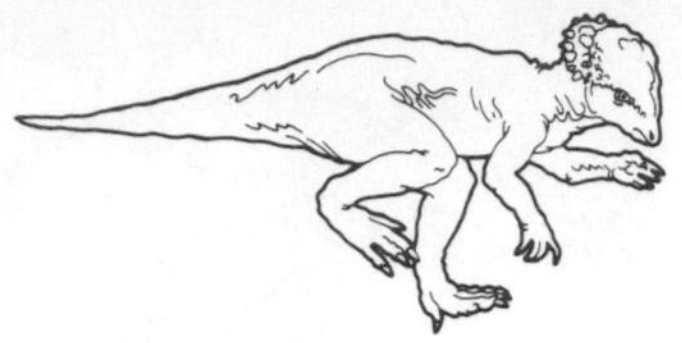

NAME: *Yaverlandia* ("Yaverland," for Yaverland Battery on the Isle of Wight, where it was found)
GROUP: Pachycephalosauria
WHEN IT LIVED: Early Cretaceous
WHERE IT LIVED: England
SIZE: Small, exact size unknown

NAME: *Pachycephalosaurus* ("thick-headed lizard")
GROUP: Pachycephalosauria
WHEN IT LIVED: Late Cretaceous
WHERE IT LIVED: Wyoming, South Dakota, Montana
SIZE: About 26 feet long

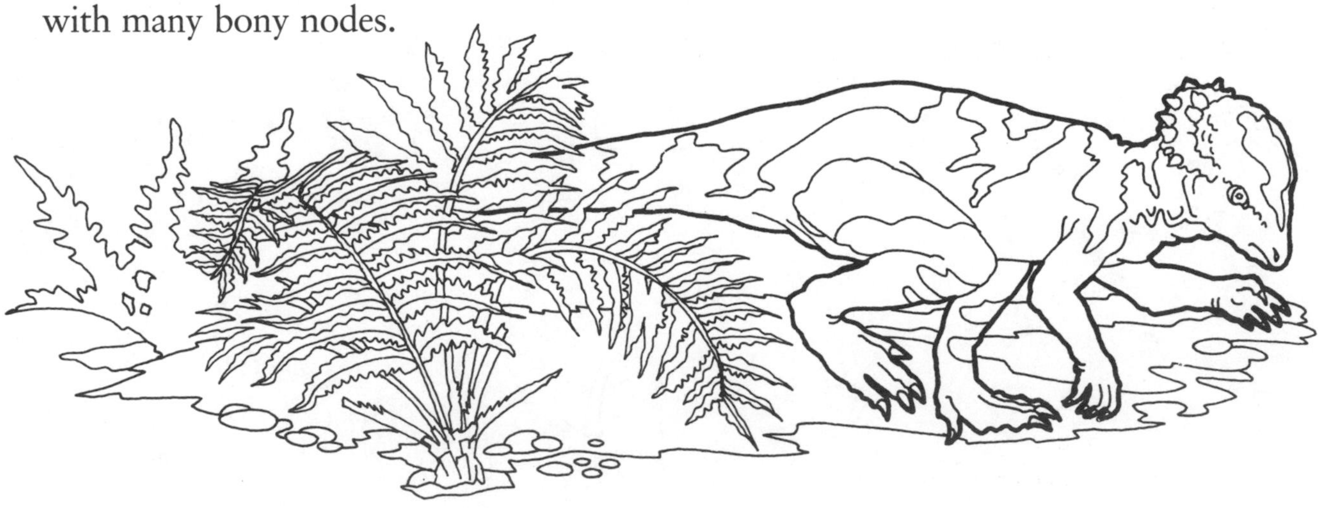

The best-known member of this group was *Stegoceras*. This dinosaur was much smaller than *Pachycephalosaurus* and had a smaller dome on its skull. Another pachycephalosaurid, *Stygimoloch,* had long spikes on its head.

What was the purpose of these thickened skull roofs and spikes? These dinosaurs probably engaged in head-to-head butting over territory or mates, as do modern-day elk. They probably did not collide head on, as most illustrations show, but banged their heads together on the sides, where there was more surface area for contact. The thickened skulls protected their brains from injury during such contests.

Dino Facts

NAME: Stegoceras ("roofed horn")

GROUP: Pachycephalosauria

WHEN IT LIVED: Late Cretaceous

WHERE IT LIVED: Alberta, Canada; Montana

SIZE: 6 feet long

NAME: Stygimoloch ("river Styx and god Moloch")

GROUP: Pachycephalosauria

WHEN IT LIVED: Late Cretaceous

WHERE IT LIVED: Montana

SIZE: Medium, exact size unknown

Horned Faces

The "horned faces," or Ceratopsia, were specialized bird-hipped dinosaurs. Except for the most primitive ones, they all had large triangle-shaped heads, with tall snouts and hooked, parrot-like horny beaks. Their heads also featured large bony frills in back and facial horns in front.

Most ceratopsians, including the well-known *Triceratops,* were heavy animals that walked on all fours—although smaller, more primitive ceratopsians walked on their hind legs only. They lived only during the Late Cretaceous and were among the last dinosaurs to die out at the end of that period.

Dino Facts

NAME: *Psittacosaurus* ("parrot lizard")

GROUP: Psittacosauridae

WHEN IT LIVED: Late Cretaceous

WHERE IT LIVED: Mongolia, China, Thailand

SIZE: 6.5 feet long

The most primitive ceratopsians belong to the group Psittacosauridae, or "parrot lizards," animals whose heads from the side resemble parrots. *Psittacosaurus*, the only known member of this group, had a body like a small ornithopod's, and like an ornithopod *Psittacosaurus* walked upright on two legs. Specimens of *Psittacosaurus* babies show that these tiny youngsters had rough teeth, indicating that they were already eating tough vegetation even as juveniles. This suggested that *Psittacosaurus,* unlike the duck-billed *Maiasaura*, was able to get its own food without help from its parents.

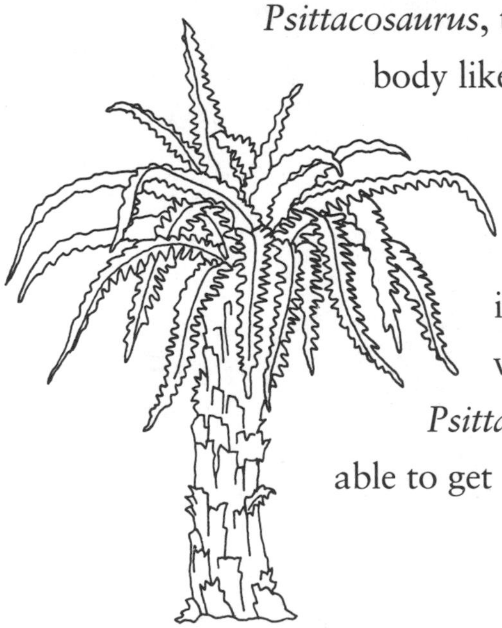

New Horned Faces

The "new horned faces," or Neoceratopsia, include all advanced ceratopsians.

The Protoceratopsidae, or "first horned faces," were a more primitive neoceratopsian subgroup and were basically hornless, though adult protoceratopsids sometimes sported raised, rough areas over their snouts and eyes. On their heads they had a bony frill, which may have evolved to house the muscles that worked its powerful jaws.

The group was named for *Protoceratops*, a small and primitive ceratopsian that already showed some features (such as its well-developed frill) that would later show up in more advanced horned dinosaurs. It also had thickened areas above its snout and eyes where prominent horns would later appear in ceratopsians.

A wide range of *Protoceratops* skulls and skeletons, from baby to adult, have been found. By comparing these specimens, we can see what changes took place in this dinosaur as it aged. One of the most noticeable changes was the growth and development of the frill. As the animal grew, its frill became wider, and its face became deeper.

Dino Facts

NAME: *Protoceratops* ("first horned face")
GROUP: Protoceratopsidae
WHEN IT LIVED: Late Cretaceous
WHERE IT LIVED: Mongolia, China
SIZE: 6 feet long, 900 pounds

NAME: *Leptoceratops* ("slender horned face")
GROUP: Protoceratopsidae
WHEN IT LIVED: Late Cretaceous
WHERE IT LIVED: Alberta, Canada; Wyoming
SIZE: 6 feet long

NAME: *Montanoceratops* ("Montana horned face")
GROUP: Protoceratopsidae
WHEN IT LIVED: Late Cretaceous
WHERE IT LIVED: Montana
SIZE: About 8 feet long

Other protoceratopsids include the more primitive *Leptoceratops* and the larger, advanced *Montanoceratops. Montanoceratops* had a more developed frill than *Protoceratops* and a much larger nose horn.

Ceratopsidae was the second, more advanced neoceratopsian group. These dinosaurs were large and mostly lived in North America. Some had huge frills and prominent face horns, and compared to all other four-legged dinosaurs, ceratopsids had the largest brains (relative to their body size).

Ceratopsids' horns were effective weapons against any carnivorous dinosaurs foolish enough to attack them. And some ceratopsid frills show wounds made by the horns of others, probably in contests over mates and territory.

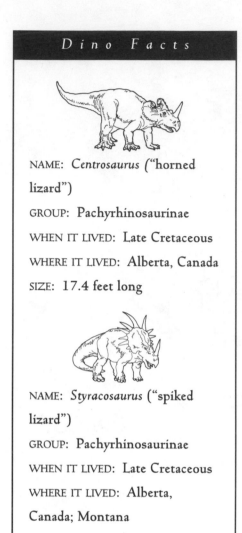

> *Dino Facts*
>
> 
>
> NAME: *Centrosaurus* ("horned lizard")
>
> GROUP: Pachyrhinosaurinae
>
> WHEN IT LIVED: Late Cretaceous
>
> WHERE IT LIVED: Alberta, Canada
>
> SIZE: 17.4 feet long
>
> 
>
> NAME: *Styracosaurus* ("spiked lizard")
>
> GROUP: Pachyrhinosaurinae
>
> WHEN IT LIVED: Late Cretaceous
>
> WHERE IT LIVED: Alberta, Canada; Montana
>
> SIZE: 18 feet long, 3 tons

The "thick nose lizards," or Pachyrhinosaurinae, had very short faces. Usually their nose horns were quite long, while their brow horns were short or nonexistent. Their frills were short, had openings (or windows, called fenestrae), and scalloped borders. Typical pachyrhinosaurines were *Centrosaurus* and *Styracosaurus.*

Centrosaurus had a pair of bony hooks pointing forward from the upper border of its frill and a long nose horn that sometimes curved forward. Numerous specimens of this dinosaur have been found in bonebeds discovered in Alberta's Dinosaur Provincial Park. This thick mass of skeletons

is really an event preserved in time. It suggests that *Centrosaurus* individuals traveled in herds, as cattle do today. This herd must have become trapped while attempting to cross a river during a flashflood. We see evidence of these magnificent animals struggling in the water, colliding with each other, and attempting to survive—only to die in the end.

Styracosaurus looked a lot like *Centrosaurus*, except for the large spikes along its frill. This spiked frill probably served the same function as the antlers of modern-day elk: The *Styracosaurus* with the largest frill

Dino Facts

NAME: *Torosaurus* ("piercing lizard")

GROUP: Ceratopsinae

WHEN IT LIVED: Late Cretaceous

WHERE IT LIVED: Wyoming, South Dakota, Utah, Texas, Colorado; Saskatchewan, Canada

SIZE: 20 feet long, 5 tons

spikes probably stood nobly at the front of his herd, proudly displaying its headgear—and using it when needed—to establish himself as the leader.

Members of the "horn faces" (Ceratopsinae) were larger and more advanced than the pachyrhinosaurines. They had long faces, short nose horns (when present), short tails, and long brow horns. Their frills were longer than those of pachyrhinosaurines and did not always have openings. Their frill borders were adorned by small bony processes called epoccipitals.

Dino Facts

NAME: *Triceratops* ("three horned face")

GROUP: Ceratopsinae

WHEN IT LIVED: Late Cretaceous

WHERE IT LIVED: Wyoming, Montana, Colorado, South Dakota; Alberta, Saskatchewan, Canada

SIZE: 25 feet long, 5 tons

The ceratopsine named *Torosaurus* had the largest head (compared to body size) of any known land animal. Its head was almost 9 feet long, almost half the length of its entire body, and most of this length was taken up by its huge 5½–foot-long frill.

The best-known and largest ceratopsine is, of course, *Triceratops*. This creature is world-famous for its short nose horn and two long brow horns. *Triceratops* had very tough skin and extremely strong jaws. Worked by muscles attached to the large neck frill, these jaws were so powerful they could bite through tree trunks!

Triceratops survived in great numbers right up to the end of the Cretaceous period. They lived at a time when many other kinds of horned dinosaurs had already died out.

It is very possible that the last dinosaur to perish on this planet was a lonely *Triceratops*.

PART FOUR:

Beyond the Bones

Skin and Color

No human being ever saw a live dinosaur, but fossils can tell us a lot about how a living dinosaur looked. A correctly assembled skeleton can show us a dinosaur's basic shape. Scars on bones indicate where and how muscles were attached. And by comparing a dinosaur's skeleton with that of a living animal we can often arrive at a reasonably accurate idea of what a dinosaur really looked like.

Sometimes a dinosaur's "soft parts," skin or scales, or impressions of them, are preserved as fossils. These also give us important information about a dinosaur's appearance. For example, we know that the hide of the horned dinosaur *Chasmosaurus* consisted of closely set, five- or six-sided small rounded processes in the skin, or tubercles, of different sizes.

The skin surface of the meat-eater *Carnotaurus* was made up of rather low, cone-shaped processes that measured from 1½ to 2 inches across. These were separated from each other by about 3 or 4 inches of small, rounded granules almost 2 inches wide.

But one thing about dinosaurs we will probably never know for certain is their color. In early pictures, dinosaurs were portrayed in drab colors, as are

some large modern animals like elephants and rhinoceroses. In most early illustrations, dinosaurs were depicted in shades of gray, green, or brown.

Today, however, paleontologists believe that dinosaurs could have been any color. Their head crests, the scales and bumps found on their skin, their frills, and their armor could have all had different tones and shades. Dinosaur skin, like the skin of modern reptiles, may have even been adorned with different-color markings, such as stripes or dots!

Today, bright colors help animals to tell each other apart and help animals of the opposite sex to attract each other. Special colors and markings can camouflage animals and can protect a peaceful herbivore from a stalking hunter or hide a hunter from its intended prey. There is no reason to think that dinosaur colors had any different function.

Whatever colors the dinosaurs were, they were examples of the natural process of adaptation to environment. By imagining the lifestyles and environments of different kinds of dinosaurs you can imagine what colors these animals may have been—and your guesses could very well be correct.

Dinosaur Traces

Dinosaurs are not only known from skeletons and body fossils—they are also known from trace fossils—preserved *traces* like footprints, eggs, and even droppings.

Much can be learned about the behavior of extinct creatures from their traces, for unlike bones, which are relics of *dead* organisms, trace fossils are records of *living* organisms, sometimes even organisms *in motion.* They are actual prehistoric moments preserved in stone. Trace fossils can give us information about ancient environments and terrain.

The most common dinosaur traces are fossil footprints, or *ichnites.* Dinosaur tracks were first found in 1836 by the Reverend Edward Hitchcock,

who believed that the three-toed fossil footprints he discovered in the Connecticut Valley were made by ancient birds. As we will soon see, Hitchcock was not that far off in his interpretation.

Footprints can tell us how fast or slow a dinosaur was, where the animal paused to rest, where it may have slipped, and where a herd of them traveled.

Interpreting dinosaur tracks is the work of a special paleontologist called an *ichnologist.* Ichnologists have made an art of learning about dinosaurs in motion from their tracks.

One famous trackway in Glen Rose, Texas, shows parallel tracks made by a sauropod and a large theropod. The sauropod trackmaker may have been *Pleurocoelus*, and the theropod *Acrocanthosaurus,* both of which lived in the time and place that these footprints were made.

The most popular interpretation of these tracks is that the theropod was stalking the sauropod—but unfortunately, the tracks do not indicate what happened if the two dinosaurs actually met.

Until recently, no fossil print had ever been positively identified as a particular dinosaur. But in 1983 a three-toed footprint measuring almost 3 feet wide was found in Upper Cretaceous rocks of New Mexico. The only large theropod known from that time and place is *Tyrannosaurus*, so there is little doubt about which dinosaur stepped into the mud many millions of years ago and left its imprint.

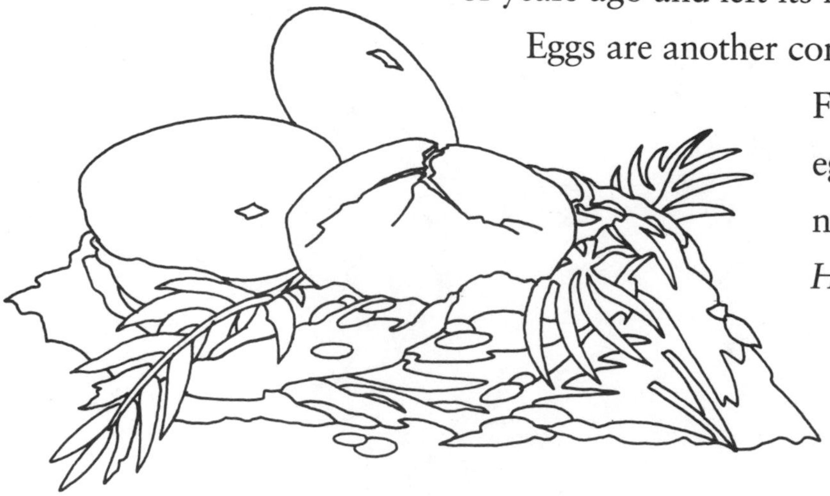

Eggs are another commonly-found dinosaur trace. Fragments of fossil dinosaur eggs were first found in 1869, near bones of the sauropod *Hypselosaurus*. The biggest egg was about twice the size of an ostrich egg. At the time,

paleontologists didn't know if the eggs belonged to the dinosaur or to some extinct bird—they were not yet certain that dinosaurs laid eggs.

The discovery of *Maiasaura* and its egg nests was important to modern thinking about dinosaurs. Until then, it was not known that dinosaurs may have had a complex social structure. With this discovery, dinosaurs became a far more interesting group of animals.

Cold-Blooded or Warm-Blooded?

For more than a century, dinosaurs were believed to be *ectothermic*, or cold-blooded, like other reptiles. Ectothermic animals take in warmth from outside sources, like the sun. As a result, they are basically sluggish creatures that spend much of their day basking in the sun, gathering heat.

In recent years, some paleontologists have proposed theories that suggest the dinosaurs were not sluggish, cold-blooded animals—that instead, they were active *endothermic* (or warm-blooded) creatures like birds and mammals that generated their own heat from within to keep their body temperature constant. A growing amount of evidence and arguments supports this idea. One of the strongest arguments is that animals with an upright stance, such as birds and mammals, need to be warm-blooded to maintain that posture. And dinosaurs walked upright; they did not sprawl and crawl like lizards.

Not all paleontologists agree, however. Much evidence indicates that dinosaurs did not need to be warm-blooded to live active lives in warm Mesozoic climates.

Were dinosaurs cold-blooded, warm-blooded, or something in-between? Were *some* dinosaurs warm-blooded? Did they begin their lives as warm-blooded hatchlings and become cold-blooded as they grew older?

Unfortunately, without a living dinosaur to examine, we may never have the answers.

But we must remember that dinosaurs were not all the same, and what is correct about the metabolism of one kind of dinosaur may not be correct about another's.

Did the Dinosaurs Die Out?

Not all dinosaurs became extinct at the same time. Various dinosaurian groups vanished gradually throughout the Mesozoic Era. Prosauropods, for example, did not survive beyond the Early Jurassic. At the end of the Cretaceous period, however, no new dinosaurian groups ever appeared.

So, why did the dinosaurs finally die out?

Dinosaur extinction may have been a very slow process, taking millions of years, with the last of the animals ultimately unable to adapt to the many changes in their world. The continents were moving (causing new wind and ocean currents, and, consequently, a cooling climate), new woodland plants were appearing that were not suited to the dinosaur diet, and even diseases were spreading as dinosaurs wandered from one land to another.

But the final extinction may have been relatively sudden, caused by some cataclysmic force—such as the collision of some giant celestial object with the Earth. According to the most popular theory, an enormous asteroid or comet, some 6 to 9 miles across, hit our planet at the end of the Cretaceous period. Supposedly, this impact created a dust cloud that darkened the sky.

This loss of sunlight killed off many of the plant species that herbivorous dinosaurs ate. This disrupted the food chain and left the plant-eaters without food. As they began to die, so did the meat-eaters that preyed on the plant-eaters. All dinosaurs perished within a short period of time—possibly years or even months.

Both extinction theories have their flaws. For example, not *all* the animals that lived at the end of the Cretaceous became extinct. Why did some animals die and not others? Also, dinosaur bones found in polar regions, where the night can last for half a year, show that these animals were perfectly adapted to surviving in long periods of darkness.

Perhaps the final extinction was the result of a number of factors working together. But, is the extinction of the dinosaurs really that important? Considering their long reign, their demise is not nearly as fascinating as their *success*.

Dinosaurs in the Air

But perhaps the dinosaurs did not die out entirely.

It has long been suspected that there was a connection between dinosaurs and birds. Remember, the first dinosaur tracks discovered were thought to be the prints of long-extinct birds.

Small, feathered *Archaeopteryx,* known from a small number of specimens, is regarded as the earliest known fossil bird. Because it had teeth and other theropod features similar to those of the tiny theropod *Compsognathus, Archaeopteryx* was first thought of as a kind of "missing link" between the Dinosauria and Aves, the group to which all birds belong.

Indeed, except for teeth, shorter arms, longer tails, and scales instead of feathers, the skeletons of many theropod dinosaurs are strikingly similar to those of *Archaeopteryx* and even modern birds.

Dino Facts

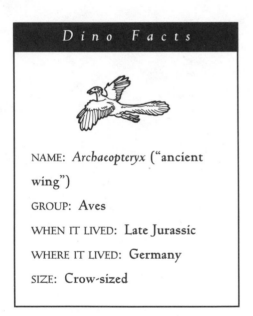

NAME: *Archaeopteryx* ("ancient wing")
GROUP: Aves
WHEN IT LIVED: Late Jurassic
WHERE IT LIVED: Germany
SIZE: Crow-sized

Today, most dinosaur paleontologists believe that birds descended from small theropods very much like *Compsognathus*. In fact, using modern methods of classification, all birds are considered to be members of the theropod group Maniraptora.

This means that *Archaeopteryx*—and all other birds, including those of today—are officially feathered dinosaurs! Remember that the next time you feed the pigeons or sit down for Thanksgiving dinner.

The idea that birds are really dinosaurs has incredible implications. There are almost 9,000 species of birds alive today. Aves is a thriving, diversified group. They live on every continent and are among the most beautiful and colorful animals on this planet. So consider this: Dinosaurs, which were thought to be extinct for 65 million years, *are still with us*.

So, at least one group of dinosaurs escaped extinction. They simply left their old domain, the ground, to conquer a new one—the sky.

In the fall, look to the skies, listen to the chirps, and watch the flocks of dinosaurs flying south for the winter.

For More Information:

Dinosaur Hunting on Your Own

Dinosaur hunting isn't only for scientists, and as this brief guide will show you, North America's dinosaur hot spots might not be too far from where you live. If you're planning a trip across the country, here are the names, locations, and numbers of several national parks, museums, and other spots throughout the United States you can visit. On with the hunt!

Location:	Name:	Activity:
Alberta, Canada	Royal Tyrrell Museum Day Digs (403) 823-7707	Fossil digs
Colorado	Denver Museum of Natural History Teen Trek (303) 370-6462	Fossil digs
Connecticut	State of Connecticut Dinosaur State Park (203) 529-5816	Fossil cast
Maryland	Calvert Marine Museum CMM Fossil Club (410) 326-2042	Fossil collecting
Montana	Smithsonian Study Tours Digging for Dinosaurs (202) 357-4800 ext. 221	Fossil digs, hikes
North Carolina	Aurora Fossil Museum Tour and Fossil Search (919) 322-4238	Lecture, fossil collecting

Texas	Fort Worth Museum of Science DinoDig (817) 732-1631	Re-created fossil dig
Utah	Dinosaurland Travel Board, Inc. Dinosaur Land (801) 789-6932	Fossil museum
Wyoming	U.S. National Park Service Fossil Butte National Monument (307) 877-4455	Hikes

The information above was excerpted from The First Annual Dinosaur Society Guide to Vacationing with the Dinosaurs. The Dinosaur Society is a nonprofit organization whose mission is to encourage dinosaur research and education. The society publishes a monthly newsletter, The Dino Times, along with encyclopedias, calendars, and other materials. For more information about The Dinosaur Society, a copy of their new catalog, or information about becoming a member, call 1-800-DINO DON, or write to:

The Dinosaur Society
200 Carelton Avenue
East Islip, NY 11730

(And if you'd like answers to difficult dinosaur questions, write to Dino Don himself at the above address.)

UNIVERSITY OF RHODE ISLAND
3 1222 01041 870 8

The Running Press Start Exploring™ Series

Color Your World

With crayons, markers and imagination, you can re-create works of art and discover the worlds of science, nature, and literature.
Each book is $8.95 and is available from your local bookstore. If your bookstore does not have the volume you want, ask your bookseller to order it for you (or send a check/money order for the cost of each book plus $2.50 postage and handling to Running Press).

ARCHITECTURE
by Peter Dobrin
Tour 60 world-famous buildings around the world and learn their stories.

BULFINCH'S MYTHOLOGY
Retold by Steven Zorn
An excellent introduction to classical literature, with 16 tales of adventure.

FOLKTALES OF NATIVE AMERICANS
Retold by David Borgenicht
Traditional myths, tales, and legends, from more than 12 Native American peoples.

FORESTS
by Elizabeth Corning Dudley, Ph.D.
Winner, *Parents' Choice* "Learning and Doing Award"
The first ecological coloring book, written by a respected botanist.

GRAY'S ANATOMY
by Fred Stark, Ph.D.
Winner, *Parents' Choice* "Learning and Doing Award"
A voyage of discovery through the human body, based on the classic work.

INSECTS
by George S. Glenn, Jr.
Discover the secrets of familiar and more unusual insects.

MASTERPIECES
by Mary Martin and Steven Zorn
Line drawings and lively descriptions of 60 world-famous paintings and their artists.

MASTERPIECES OF AMERICAN ART
From the National Museum of American Art, Smithsonian Institution
by Alan Gartenhaus
Sixty ready-to-color masterpieces and their stories, including contemporary works.

OCEANS
by Diane M. Tyler and James C. Tyler, Ph.D.
Winner, *Parents' Choice* "Learning and Doing Award"
An exploration of the life-giving seas, in expert text and 60 pictures.

PLACES OF MYSTERY
by Emmanuel M. Kramer
An adventurous tour of the most mysterious places on Earth, with more than 50 stops along the way.

SPACE
by Dennis Mammana
Share the discoveries of history's greatest space scientists and explorers.